forgetting

Forgetting

Frederika Amalia Finkelstein

TRANSLATED BY ISABEL COUT
AND CHRISTOPHER ELSON

DEEP VELLUM PUBLISHING
DALLAS, TEXAS

Deep Vellum Publishing
3000 Commerce St., Dallas, Texas 75226
deepvellum.org · @deepvellum

Deep Vellum is a 501c3 nonprofit literary arts organization
founded in 2013 with the mission to bring
the world into conversation through literature.

FIRST EDITION, 2023

Support for this publication was provided in part by grants from the National Endowment
for the Arts, Amazon Literary Partnership, the Ackerman Center for Holocaust Studies, the
Texas Commission on the Arts, City of Dallas Office of Arts & Culture, and the George &
Fay Young Foundation.

LIBRARY OF CONGRESS CATALOGING-IN-PUBLICATION DATA

Names: Finkelstein, Frederika Amalia, author. | Cout, Isabel, translator. |
  Elson, Christopher, 1965- translator.
Title: Forgetting / Frederika Amalia Finkelstein ; translated by Isabel
  Cout and Christopher Elson.
Other titles: Oubli. English
Description: First edition. | Dallas, Texas : Deep Vellum Publishing, 2023.
Identifiers: LCCN 2023018768 | ISBN 9781646052264 (trade paperback) | ISBN
  9781646052523 (ebook)
Subjects: LCSH: Holocaust, Jewish (1939-1945)—Fiction. | LCGFT:
  Psychological fiction. | Novels.
Classification: LCC PQ2706.I557 O9313 2023 | DDC 843/.92—dc23/
eng/20230428
LC record available at https://lccn.loc.gov/2023018768

ISBN (TPB) 978-1-64605-226-4 | ISBN (Ebook) 978-1-64605-252-3

Cover design by David Wojciechowski

Interior layout and typesetting by KGT

PRINTED IN CANADA

*To the memory of my grandfather, Jacobo
and to my brother, Stanislas*

One more time
DAFT PUNK

The absence of solution is inexpressible
GEORGES BATAILLE

I will not reveal my most intimate feelings
ADOLF EICHMANN

I

1

Extermination of the Jews. I won't get into the details—
you've already been force-fed them *ad nauseam*, had
horrible things inflicted on you like *Night and Fog*,
infusing your mind with a miserable sense of guilt. I say
this without shame: I want to forget, to annihilate that
vile Shoah from my memory, and to extract it from my
brain like a tumor. I want the abyss of History to swallow it forever.

I keep hoping the dead are going to leave me in
peace, but that seems futile. A vision of the showers
in Auschwitz after the SS have released the Zyklon B
comes to trouble me at night when I can't sleep. The
scene unfolds about three to ten minutes after the dis-
persal of the gas through those slits in the walls which
have been designed for massacre. I smell something
acrid, I see bodies, white and naked, heaped on top
of one another. There are children, women, old people; they form piles of human flesh. Those highest up

scratched at the ceiling with such intensity they left their nails embedded in it. All their heads are shaved, but, on the backs of necks neglected by razors, some hairs still remain, coarse as straw. Most of the individuals succumbed with their eyes open, staring off at some point in the void. The coughs, the groans, the suffocating—it has all ceased. Nothing remains but the silence of death.

I've forgotten the date of the day I'm living. I get up and sit on my bed, back against the wall. I wonder out loud to the voice recognition software on my phone what day it is. A female voice (her name is Siri, she sounds like a blonde) answers that today is Sunday, April 25, and that it's 2:30 AM. I tell her: "Siri, I'm afraid to sleep," but she pretends not to understand me. I press my white earbuds into my ears. "One More Time" starts playing quietly. The song does its job, I'd say it even provokes the urge to dance slowly in my room—I succeed perfectly at chasing the vision from my mind. I turn up the volume. The repetitive rhythm drowns out the voice inside me that says it's an illusion to think I'll ever really be able to forget Zyklon B and those necks neglected by razors. I can affirm with certainty that my grandfather did not die in Auschwitz, and this fact should be enough to free me from my phobia of showers.

Sometimes I fall into bitterness. That's when I'm

tempted to confide my feelings in a machine. Even in today's world, the emotional capacities of machines remain unsatisfying: there's a lack of warmth. It's possible this problem will soon be resolved—I'm counting on progress to bring us the scientific conquest of emotion. I don't know if that's likely, just as I don't know whether the day science is able to make machines truly capable of emotion will also be the last day of humanity (there is the effect, and its cause). I think our world is organized to perfection; from this point of view, we could say it's a masterpiece, a chef d'oeuvre. It only falls short in one respect: I'd like to be able to confide in a machine capable of feeling.

What would you say if I claimed that this deficiency might be the price to be paid for having eradicated approximately 14,000,000 human beings in the space of twelve years, about 6,000,000 of which were Jews? Why not imagine? Gas, firing squads, starvation—all in the most extraordinarily organized manner, the consequence being that I'll no doubt never be allowed to interact with a machine capable of emotion. There was a choice to be made: ravage humanity or create machines capable of feeling—and that choice was made. This is only one hypothesis, I have many. Sometimes, though, my eyes fill with tears when I'm in front of my Mac, but of course my Mac has never had its eyes fill with tears in front of me. It's condemned to the absence of tears, something which, now that I think about it—and it's just a passing thought—was probably made possible by the circulation of Zyklon B through the lungs of Jews, homosexuals, the disabled, the insane: I could go on. It should be noted that "One More Time" is a perfectly composed piece of music, by which I mean that the absence of feeling is carried to its highest degree of mastery.

I have my whole life before me: in other words, I shouldn't be being crushed beneath an avalanche of dark thoughts. But I can't help it, I tell myself that maybe one day I'll wake up and have forgotten everything. When I say everything I mean: music, the color of the sky, the taste of Coke, my grandfather's face (I only have two pictures), the hatred and the love, too, my memories, and the little I've learned. Why am I afraid to sleep? Well that's just it—to sleep is to run the risk of losing everything. *I could wake up tomorrow with my memory blank* is the thought that comes to poison my rest every night, and I am possessed with a fear which delays the moment when I could deliver myself from the weightiness of waking life and from this tiredness accumulated over interminable hours. At regular intervals, I think it: *this next second could be the second I lose my memory*. If it's possible for a computer, it has to be possible for a human.

If I start to lose, I'll only keep losing. It's an art, and

I know it in the way only those who lose things know: losing, like winning, is a spiral. The world has a perfect logic, like I've already said, and that's exactly what I admire about it. This ruthless logic is the only law of our world, and that's how it will be until the end.

∞∞∞∞

I open my Mac. Done with Auschwitz. Suddenly, I see Times Square at night on my screensaver, and the image remains before my eyes for several seconds. It sucks me in: I forget what was bothering me in the space of a moment. My computer is there to choose what belongs in my memory, and in this respect, I can affirm that technology is fabulous—not to mention, it came along at just the right time. I love it to a degree that's inexpressible (it goes without saying this love contains an aspect of hatred). It's there for me when I'm alone in the face of all these morbid thoughts. When I'm not doing well, when I feel shitty, when I'm raw from loneliness: I open my computer, it's already on, I go online and a new adventure begins.

I repeat: I have absolutely no fear of forgetting the extermination of the Jews. More specifically, I want to be left in peace, not have to deal with it anymore, for it to be cut out of my life once and for all because that's the only way I can survive. I cannot bear the bludgeoning to which our society continually subjects itself, I cannot bear what is inflicted on my brain starved for hope and gentleness. I want to live in a world without violence, neutral and harmonious like Switzerland (at least, Switzerland as I dream it to be), and I want to be able to listen to Daft Punk without thinking of the hair of women, shaved and gathered in jars next to other jars filled with the teeth, nails, skin of Jews, without thinking of the dead who disgust me simply because they were exterminated. *They are rats*, killed like rats! I want to see the sun rise before 7:00 AM just because I love spring for the beauty of its dawn alone, I want to wander around the Place des Vosges until day emerges from night without a single sinister thought to disturb me. Soon, I'll go out and watch the sunrise, then I'll wander on foot all the way to rue d'Hauteville and I'll go to bed in silence.

You don't even know who I am

Nice to meet you—my name is Alma, I'm somewhere between twenty and twenty-five years old. Alma-Dorothéa is my real name, but everyone's called me Alma since I was a teenager because ever since then, when I've been asked "What's your name?", I've settled for just saying: *Alma*, and hiding the rest. When I was a kid, they called me Dorothéa, but I want to forget the child I was forever. We want to forget the things in us that are torn. Call me whatever you'd like—I'll let you name me.

∞∞∞

Let's get back to business. Some disagree with the numbers. Some re-count the dead. Numbers demand a commitment and a rigor that can be sickening if you have even a slight predisposition to thoroughness. In other words, numbers isolate us: I know this because they haunt me. I think I can say the Nazis suffered from an extreme solitude, the loneliness of calculation. The whole world now lives on top of this immense stratum of Nazi solitude that makes up our ground: the immense loneliness of numbers. Sometimes I wish I could leave it behind, if only for a couple hours. I want to go to sleep some night without thinking of a date or of a number. I'd like to savor the moment I'm in. My memory has turned on me, it has stopped absorbing time—I forget nearly everything, then I remember, and then I forget again. Everything but the sounds and the numbers, dutifully steadfast. One day someone asked me if my grandfather died in Auschwitz. I answered: "No, in Buchenwald." Sometimes I find myself lying. The real reason why escapes me. It's 2:45 AM, I'm at home and I'm alone because at night I want to be able to construct an explanation or a reasoning, as feeble and twisted as it might be. I need a moment of intellectual peace, to swim in a river of thoughts, neutral or obscure, to wander on the other side of all the closed circuits. "One More Time" restarts in my headphones, I think of Glenn Gould's Goldberg Variations, of their coldness. I regularly experience an unease when I listen to music: the overlaying of multiple melodies in my mind, like the layering of bodies in a ditch (I use lots of metaphors)—that same disorder, minus the filth and the putrefaction. When that Daft Punk song blared in my ears again a couple of minutes ago, I heard the second movement of Schubert's twenty-first sonata. Many music-loving Nazis must have cried when they heard it. Sleep doesn't come anywhere near me, I don't feel tired at all, I even feel like I could go running in a T-shirt out in the cold night, all the way to the banks of the Seine. I know I could, and that's reason enough to rid me of the need. I could die an athlete's sudden death—that's a risk I'd like to avoid. My grandfather was born in 1912, the same year as Eva Braun. On the twelfth of December, not January first (that's the day he died). He was born December 12, 1912, in Krakow, Poland.

To be completely honest with you, I don't know why I pretended my grandfather died in a camp. I said: "No, in Buchenwald," and I lied. I eat an apple, trying to remember the names of the Nazi concentration and extermination camps—I need to remember. I know the main ones, I learned them off by heart a few years ago, to settle the question. There's a very handy map on Wikipedia. The legend includes two symbols: a black death's head for the extermination camps and a red death's head for the concentration camps—the same little symbol you find on bottles of detergent. I learned the names of the camps in alphabetical rather than geographical order because it's simpler and neater in my head. My apple has six seeds, I spit them out—a disgusting habit. I begin. Auschwitz I, Auschwitz II, Auschwitz III (the easiest ones to remember), Bad Sulza, Belzec, Bergen-Belsen, Chelmno, Dachau, Dora, Esterwegen, Flossenbürg, Fuhlsbüttel, Groß-Rosen, Hertogenbosch, Hinzert, Kaunas, Klooga, Lichtenburg, Lublin-Majdanek, Maly Trostenëts, Mauthausen, Moringen, Natzweiler-Struthof, Neuengamme, Niederhagen-Wewelsburg, Oranienburg, Ravensbrück, Riga-Kaiserwald, Sachsenburg, Sobibor, Treblinka, Vaivara. Thirty-two camps, built, used, and abandoned, over a period of eight years, between 1937 and 1945. Thirty-two is the number I remember. It's painful for me to admit this list is incomplete, by which I mean: imperfect. This obsession with numbers gnaws at me, working away in me—sometimes I'm afraid it's killing me. I am obsessed with this word, "work." In the camps too, they worked. Work was one of my family's essential values,

I think it probably is in all families. I know the risks I run with all this, one of these days: madness or suicide. I need to care for myself, but I don't know how . . . Maybe I don't know anything. My eyes focus on a lightbulb hanging from the ceiling of my room. I say to myself: it's possible this world has no logic, that everything is the result of pure, meaningless chance. No logic at all. The intensity of the light has left an imprint on my pupils, I see a white spot wherever I look. A nervous laugh ripples through my body. Now there's an extremely disturbing thought. And yet, I'm drawn to it. I've always imagined a logical world because I've always trusted in numbers. Numbers adhere to an implacable logic. It's this rigor that I love, that I approve of, that I bow to. Numbers can never betray me; at worst, they'll surprise me in an unpleasant way, but they'll never fail at their task. They'll continue to fulfill their duty, tirelessly and eternally. "Did your grandfather die in Auschwitz?"— "No, in Buchenwald." I lied. Why? I hated the question. It was tone deaf.

One night last week, I heard this phrase on TV: "Every day I pass through death." I liked it. I look at my watch, it's now 3:12 AM. Every day, my watch falls five more minutes behind because it was made sixty years ago, when Adolf Eichmann was still alive. I haven't adjusted it in forty-eight hours. So in reality it's 3:22 AM. I wonder at what point I started to see living as a constant threat. I can envisage three possibilities. First: a radical reversal may have taken place at a particular moment, translatable into a particular date, time, year, and I just wasn't paying attention properly in that instant and missed it. Second: a gradual stalemate, not traceable to a discrete moment, but with a calculable correspondence to a certain period (I don't know which one) during my twenty-something years of existence. Third: my whole life has always been a nightmare, since the moment I began living. Is laying this out useful? No. I have to let go of these poisonous parasite-thoughts that distract me from my goal. I probably lie more than I think I do, but I'm not sure just how much. My memory is torn apart—a thousand little pieces dispersed through time. My family hid a lot of details from me, families always have an aversion to details (genealogy is regrettably no longer their strong suit). I am preceded by three-quarters of nothingness. The only thing that remains is the life of my grandfather, known to me only a little, simply because he was his daughter's hero. My grandfather's life was relayed to me mythically, with lots of numbers and data. I'm under no illusions: so many of the facts they told me are certainly lies. It doesn't matter, it's not even an issue for me. I don't attach much importance to facts. Truth is not a story of facts—it is everything it wants to be.

When I'm tense, I do some mental math to ease

my mind. I have a glass in my right hand but it's empty because there's nothing to drink at my place. An empty glass is entirely imperfect, and therefore unsettling. I know the number of imperfection: it's the number 6. A weariness comes over me. I'm thirsty. I think back to the worst moments of my childhood, to the ways I was coerced by my brother, only able to fill my glass with Coke if I caved to his petty blackmail. Some lives are poisoned. Time accelerates and expands. I go back to my computer. My eyes linger on the homepage of the largest search engine in the world, hypnotized by its whiteness and its purity. I was eight years old, I was sitting on the wood floor, hands on my knees. My brother said, "Listen." I felt these vibrations in my throat, and then a cold and genderless voice was repeating "One More Time." The song replays in my headphones, my eyes glued to the screen. I think the release of *Discovery* has to be one of the most important moments in my life and in History. There's nothing left to eat, nothing left to drink, tap water disgusts me. I stay sitting on a transparent chair for several minutes, mentally collapsed. I wonder what I'm going to do tonight, more precisely, the question is: how to hold on until dawn? I turn toward my black piano, pushed up against the wall, cloaked in dust. The cover is locked, and it's been several months since I lost the key. A feeling of nausea comes over me. "I'd like to play piano. I don't play piano, and I never will, that fact suffocates me, sometimes even more than the horrors, the black river of my past which carries me through the years. I literally can't get over it." One day, I read that in a novel, and my eyes suddenly interrupted their reading because I, too, will literally never recover, never make up for giving up on the piano. Glenn Gould never gave up on it: that demonstrates a courage he can be proud of. Daft Punk stops playing, and SebastiAn begins, my ears burn. Dawn is going to come at 6:40 AM. A pale light will enter my room. I open the window and gently reach my hand outside, it's not very cold out, the street is as empty and quiet as the sky. I close the window and my eyes fall upon a crack: I watch the wall splinter. My memory, my brain, time, and the world are all like this crack. It's no illusion. Adolf Hitler hated cracks. He would have had this wall repainted immediately.

ooooo

I am swept along by something obscene. I don't understand why, it's just something I know. I want to fill my glass with Coke, right now that's the only thing I want. I have to tell you that I refused water for a long time. Its clarity was unbearable to me. As a child, I drank only Coke. Once, I went forty-eight hours without drinking because there was no Coke in the house. A dehydrated body becomes delirious. It's a unique experience. Your head swells with pain, your mouth becomes dry and sour, your gaze modifies its own vision. You see strange landscapes, the contours catch fire, and then you get cold, you tremble and start to laugh. Dehydration played a crucial role in the camps. Some prisoners died swallowing their own tongues, incapacitated by extreme thirst. Water was made into a scarce resource in order to dessicate the bodies of prisoners, draining them progressively of all substance right down to their last tear. Water was readily available, however, for the so-called medical experiments. They plunged "subjects" into baths of freezing water. Doctor Sigmund Rascher wrote to Himmler on April 5, 1942, describing a series of "aquatic" experiments performed at Dachau. I learned several lines off by heart. "The *subjects* were submerged into the water with all the equipment on, including the headband. A lifejacket kept them afloat. The temperature of the water varied from two to eleven degrees celsius. During the first experiments, the cerebellum and the back of the neck were kept out of the water. Over the course of other experiments, the back of the neck and the cerebellum were submerged. We electrically recorded temperatures of 26.5 degrees celsius in the stomach, and 26.6 degrees celsius in the rectum. Death occurred only once the cold reached the spinal cord and the cerebellum." I was plagued by the obsessive fear that my grandfather could have died in conditions like these. So I learned these sentences to rationally contain the experiments in my memory in case he had endured them to avoid letting my imagination wander beyond the strict facts. It has to be said that the presence of numbers simplified this task for me.

I sit down on the wood floor, back against the couch. My foot bumps against a book. On the cover, the icy gaze of Talleyrand. I open it to the page with the epigraphs. I read: *God (or the devil) is in the details.* I wonder what he would have chosen in 1940—Vichy or London? I don't know the limits of a man with the blood of a Bourbon on his hands. No more than I know my own. Undeniably, it's the absence of limits that harms me. Always more calculations. Always more dates. Always more numbers. Always more music. Always more nightmares. Always more all-nighters. It's 4:12 AM, the morning is coming and I tell myself that soon the dead will be behind me. Sometimes I venture naive thoughts in an excess of hopefulness. I hate my weaknesses, but I close my eyes.

ooooo

A little while ago, I decided that I would permit myself everything. Who, on a given day, was not awed to learn that 6,000,000 Jews were exterminated in the space of

6 years? Let's define the term *awed*: with horror before an abomination, with surprise, with sadness, with anger, with fear, with disgust—each with a certain passion, you could say. The number 6,000,000 does not sink in, any human reason capable of emotion cannot accept it. This number remains in the doorway, at the threshold: it is inadmissible. In the face of 6,000,000, there are three options: forget the number, modify the number, deny the number. Moreover, to 6,000,000 I could add the number 8, in reference to the other 8,000,000 non-Jews exterminated on European soil between 1933 and 1945. But see, I'm not going to. Why? Because my story is linked to 6,000,000, that's to say, the story of my ancestors. The number 6,000,000 outweighs the number 8,000,000: it is a question of having been assigned. Try as I might to deny it, I will remain assigned to the number 6,000,000 until the end of my days. I didn't say I wouldn't be able to distance myself from it—that's one of the reasons I haven't hung myself yet. I said that I'd remain assigned to that number. I must admit, rather painfully, that the number 8, unlike the number 6 with its diabolical connotations, might have been simpler (would you even know if I were lying?) but go on the internet, open a history book: you'll find 6,000,000 Jews. The number 6 cannot be ignored.

ooooo

Truth be told, when I can't sleep, I go on Google Images and look at black and white photos of old baseball teams. I scan each face, thinking: *he's dead*. All you need to do is look up "vintage baseball team." That's when I realize this has always been my destiny. I need to do this research to remind myself I'm going to die one day—a detail I tend to forget. That's what I'm doing now. I type in "vintage baseball team," I press *enter*, and, instantly, I see them. They're resplendent. Distinguished; proud; eternal; unforgettable.

If I want to really commit, I need to renounce any kind of morality. No morality means no humanism either—that's an idea I advise you to accept. Instead, I believe in numbers: everyone has to believe in something (it's not as though we have a choice). Yes, I called them *rats*. How could I? I could cry about it, but I'm incapable since I feel no sadness—only disgust. If anything, it would be shame that would make me puke, thinking of those miserable, humiliating deaths, but curiously I feel no shame. It's more like an irrepressible existential anxiety, and fortunately mental math is there to help me unwind, and my baseball teams, or, if I have the energy, a little game of chess with myself. I told myself I could just visit a slaughterhouse, no need to go all the way to Auschwitz. It's 4:32 AM now and I'm not even hungry. I could call a friend, suggest we get a drink. But to those who sleep badly, rest is precious: I'm afraid to wake people. I'm even more afraid of waking them on a Sunday. I listen to "One More Time" one last time. Tonight, I don't tire of it. I want to say, just between us, that death and love are the two words that preoccupy me more than anything else in the world.

2

· The aristocrats and the Jews must be eliminated
REINHARD HEYDRICH

The memory of yesterday visits me in the night. It was
the morning: yesterday morning. It was Saturday, the
most extraordinary day of the week. I don't know how
long I stood before the window of the Louis Vuitton
store on the Champs-Élysées. The resin mannequins
sparkled as though with a thousand little flames: their
cleanness seduced me. I remember thinking for a
moment about the employee who had probably pol-
ished the mannequins with the help of a disinfectant
wipe, ridding the whole surface of up to 99.9 percent of bacteria—another human feat I bow to, even if
the number doesn't quite reach 100 percent. Speakers
played an ethereal and mellifluous melody that sounded
like Mahler's Sixth Symphony, so much so that for an
instant I thought I was dreaming. It wasn't Mahler. In
the center of the store display, between two mannequins,

there was a TV screen: I saw clouds pass beneath a crepuscular sky of orange and pink, as though I was looking out the window of an airplane. I couldn't say why, but I have to confess that I was transported by those images. It was a video of the sky over Paris and, little by little, as the camera descended, you could see the zinc rooftops, a red and white hot-air balloon on the horizon. It was romantic. I seem to recall thinking: *I don't want to leave, I want to enter this world. I want to enter the universe of Louis Vuitton, to live beneath its orange and pink sky.* The installation had moved me, I felt something like an emotion—an occurrence that happens to me less and less these days. It has become very difficult for me to feel an emotion: that's why I stay open to all possibilities.

When I went into the Publicis drugstore to buy a can of Pepsi later, I was still thinking of Louis Vuitton and his pink and orange sky. I stole his sky, or maybe he had stolen my imagination, it doesn't matter—in any event, I can now say I've got a new sky. Orange, pink, a red and white hot-air balloon, those rooftops, the Louvre, the carefreeness, the sweetness of it all. The number 6,000,000 was far away. In that orange sky, there were no numbers. No crowd, the Place de la Concorde was empty, there was only sky as far as the eye could see, a sky of perfect purity: no human beings—that's exactly what I liked about it. I was in the store when I remembered that

I'd forgotten my headphones. I came out of the Publicis with a can of Pepsi in hand, listening to the sounds of the city. The sky was gray. Paris was in the process of covering over the sun. I've noticed that there were way more yellow rays around during my childhood, about ten years ago. I could waste time proving it, but it's not worth the energy, since it's already obvious that everything must come to an end. I won't reopen the question of that law, which I came to accept several years ago (I didn't always believed in the inevitability of endings). The weather in the capital doesn't really frighten me, all of that stuff is calculated: we are in decline.

I walked without stopping. I wanted to avoid sitting and thinking about the future. About people, about school, about lack of love, about this life that I must not waste. I really am afraid of wasting my life. I tell myself over and over that I need to do better: I need to accomplish something much larger than myself. To be more precise, I think about it in these terms: *I need to commit to things, I have to go all the way.* I don't know where the *have to, need to* comes from, and that doesn't interest me. It's a desire that probably doesn't make any sense. No one goes all the way, like I already said: everything is calculated.

I can't allow myself the right to be afraid or to ask questions about the origin of all of this. I have to only think about the necessity of my success, regardless of whether it's an illusion or not. I'd like to be left in peace with these illusions about my life and the world, at least for a couple more years. Succeed, in French *réussir*, coming from the Latin *exire*: to leave. I want to leave and never come home. I continued to walk along the Champs-Élysées, surrounded by tourists and PSG supporters. A Ferrari flashed before my eyes. It was a red Modena 360. The light was green, I ran. The red reminded me of something. It took me a couple seconds to figure out what exactly, then I thought of the video game GTA Vice City for Playstation 2: I remembered driving an incalculable number of red Ferraris in that game, red Ferraris and orange Lamborghinis and yellow Hummers. I was still thirsty, I was afraid. I no longer really knew where I was. The Modena's red had so completely saturated my memory that I'd completely lost my bearings. *Where am I?* I thought. *I am in front of the Cartier store.* It took me a second to understand that sentence. I was still seeing that saturated red. I think I heard "Billie Jean" by Michael Jackson, but playing backward. That wasn't coming from the street, it was coming from inside my head. In GTA, a modder had configured it so that "Billie Jean" started playing whenever you got into a car. I've driven a lot of cars in that game. I've heard a lot of "Billie Jean." I was in front of the Arc de Triomphe; my can was empty. And then I had a desire. I really wanted something, but what was it? Impossible to remember.

ooooo

I said I was between twenty and twenty-five years old. I won't divulge my exact age, because that age will have changed already by the time I reread the sentence. Ages lie. I don't believe in them and never will. Maybe that's a mistake. It's not that numbers lie, but that ages do, because skin ages in a constant, uninterrupted way: pores expand in real time. I ended up ratifying this law, too. I could count my dilated pores every morning; that's a task I could definitely see myself doing. But I decided that there had to be a limit to my obsessiveness, so I decided not to start counting my pores. Not to learn that number by heart. Not to wake up every morning, waiting to be able to say that the number has increased in the last twenty-four hours. Limits are fundamental in that they ground the life of all beings. In my case, my excessiveness is still guided and contained by a certain mental discipline. Refusing to calculate the number of dilated pores on my face is one example of a limit (there are some others).

Alma, come back

Supermarkets are one of the important places from my childhood. I always ended up running away and getting lost in the aisles. I'd hear: "Dorothéa, come back!" To this day, I regularly change cereal brands. The toy hidden inside doesn't interest me, it never did: I am completely absorbed by the variation in colors. Every week a new box. Nestle or Kellogg's? It all depends on which one does the most to attract my attention. When I enter a supermarket, I always think: *They did it.* They made the calculations, and those calculations have held up. They went all the way. I dream of a supermarket that never closes. We're behind on that one—America has already made that dream a reality. But it's only a matter of time. Soon, I'll be able to walk into the supermarket on rue d'Hauteville at 3:30 AM to buy a box of Kellogg's and a bottle of Coke while listening to Daft Punk. The perfection of that sentence touches me: it's a particular kind of radical. I'd like to cry tears of Coke so I could drink them. It's night now. I just left my apartment because the loneliness was suffocating me.

ooooo

Now I'm on rue d'Hauteville, right outside my building. It's Sunday morning, around 4:45 AM, and I just drifted away for a few seconds in order to remember what I did with my Saturday.

My name is Alma. My hair is light brown, streaked with gold in the sunlight. I have dark eyes, they're walnut-colored, even hinting at dark green on nice days.

My skin is pale, my eyes are almond-shaped, I'm wearing a pair of American Apparel jeans, blue as a May sky, and a white T-shirt of unknown age and origin (it's from that category of clothing generally kept secret, what we might call an undershirt), and I'm saving the best for last: my hunting jacket, dark as my eyes, and smelling faintly of tar. I wore it the day my dog was buried, and since then it's been legendary to me.

I close my eyelids for a moment. I know that I'm in Paris just by inhaling deeply and tasting: the wind in Paris has a singular flavor, like the wind of every city. The taste of the wind varies according to geographical position: the north wind is different from the south wind.

I think it must be around 4:45 AM, I couldn't say the exact time—I took off my watch before I went out—and I know that soon I'm going to leave this street, but to go where? I've made the decision now, and to me, that's the only thing that matters. I think that I want everything, want so much to the point that I want nothing. Who else thinks like this, like me? I want to question them all, all the humans in the world, and then the animals. If we were only able to question dogs, cats, and horses: just those three species, that would be enough. I told myself that maybe I'd go see a horse race tomorrow morning (which is now today—this morning). The Grand Steeple-Chase de Paris is an event I wouldn't miss for anything in the world, and it's happening today.

The universe of the racetrack is nothing new to me. I lived across from the Auteuil Hippodrome when I was a kid (not so long ago), so I rarely missed the big race. All I needed was a pair of binoculars to see the track from my house. I think I can walk all the way to the racetrack. If I leave now, I'll probably be in Auteuil in one hour if I walk quickly, or maybe two hours, even three if I really take my time. The advantage of going slowly is that by the time I get there, the sun will already be up: I'll have the joy of seeing the little burst of early sunlight over the stadium, and there'll be enough light to illuminate the empty racecourse. I won't wear a hat and I can always listen to Daft Punk to distract myself from the fact that I'm poorly dressed: my headphones are in the right pocket of my jeans.

Otherwise, I could stay here, on rue d'Hauteville, and build a virtual racetrack in my mind with the most beautiful horses and the silkiest, greenest grass. I could imagine the whole steeplechase course, reproduce it in my head. I saw lots of horses in my childhood: Thoroughbreds, Anglo-Arabians—their coats any number of colors (chestnut, black, bay, etc). Modeling the racehorses in my mind off of chestnut Thoroughbreds and bay Anglo-Arabians, it would be entirely possible for my imagination to produce the race, the only condition being that I'll have to redouble my concentration on following them over the course itself: imaginary races are more difficult for the brain to follow, since it requires so much exertion for the mind to stage continuous movement. What do you think about adding a baseball diamond in a big, empty green space next to the racetrack? I figure, I love baseball, why deprive myself? A baseball game and horse race happening simultaneously. Bats, gloves, players, jockeys, jumbotron, home-run, steeplechase.

I'm going to add baseball

I've been saying all of this stuff in the hope that it will make me forget the moment I'm actually living. It's night, I'm walking down rue d'Hauteville with the dead as my only companions. I'm surrounded by some members of the SS and a few baseball players, we are stepping over naked bodies piled on top of one another, and the sickening smell of Auschwitz's chimneys, of sulfur and death, is tightening its grip around our throats. I can never manage to be really alone, which means I'm alone in the world.

The dead follow me. I don't know where they come from or what they want. They can materialize suddenly, at any moment, day or night. Look, they're here right now. They come up beside me as I watch TV, when I'm playing video games, or turning the pages of a book; they are at my bedside as I fall asleep; they're there at my horse races and my baseball games. The dead don't sit—they remain standing to observe the victories and the defeats.

The dead invade my thoughts, my visions, my dreams: I don't know how to get rid of them. In truth, I'd like to tell them that I'm listening, in the hope that they'll turn around and leave me in peace, but I don't know if they can hear me. They're mute, they don't smile: they don't react at all. I don't know why they come, I don't know what they could want from me, the only thing I can say is that I see them in black and white. It's possible that my mind has assigned to them the faces of those baseball players that pop up on Google Images when I search: "vintage baseball team." It's equally possible that the faces from the identification photos of Jews who died in the camps have stayed with me, since I've seen hundreds of them—also on the internet, on different commemorative sites for victims of the Shoah. I'm not exactly fascinated by the faces of the dead: it's more of a sensitivity. And I don't know what there is to be embarrassed about—it's no doubt even a *healthy* thing to be sensitive in this way. Consider this: it's other people who should be embarrassed, the ones who are afraid to look upon the faces of the dead. It's they who are sick, because they're afraid of those faces which remind them they have yet to cross over to that other shore (I mean to cross from the shore of life to the shore of death). They're afraid of what no longer belongs to their world, and I understand them. There truly is something to fear—something to make us shudder.

ooooo

Why do we have to die? That's the eternal question. I won't take the bait, since we already know no one's in a position to give us an answer. In the face of "Why do we have to die?", every response and every speech produces the exact same effect: they drop like flies. But I can sidestep that trap with one simple statement that I'll repeat as many times as necessary—until my hatred of the verb "to die" evaporates and there remains not even the faintest memory of the distress it once caused: I'll repeat that time is an illusion.

Incidentally, I don't even need to come up with an inevitably pathetic response to the question of "Why do we have to die?" because I have my baseball games. And my baseball games and my steeplechases, imaginary and eternal as they are, spit in the face of dying. My imagination is a stronghold; inside it, I am all-powerful, no one can harm me. So I do what I want with time: I go back, I press pause, I fast-forward whenever I want, as though I were indestructible when inside my mind. It's true that the dead are there too, but they don't pose any threat. They've never said a word to me, certainly never that I ought to join them: they simply watch me.

Last night I listened to jazz for at least six hours. I couldn't sleep. I couldn't stand any more Daft Punk or Mahler or Glenn Gould, but I was afraid of silence. I've never been able to finish reading *The Critique of Pure Reason*, but it remains on my bedside table. Maybe I should have begun by saying that my grandfather died with *The Critique of Pure Reason* beside him—a detail that came back to me in the moment when I was drawing up my imaginary racetrack and baseball field in front of my apartment, at 58 rue d'Hauteville (fourth floor; no elevator; a horrible, suffocating little room), while I drank a Pepsi with bubbles so delicate, so lightly acidic they burst on my palate like a sudden rain showers a pastoral landscape, or maybe a forest.

Every once in a while, I'd drink Coke while walking through the forest; the Compiègne forest, the Fontainebleau forest, and also on the beach at Deauville, my bare feet venturing onto warm sand, damp and compact—my Labrador retriever running on that sand made wet by water from the sky and from the waves. I've never slept so much anywhere as I did at Deauville. I went once: it was a week before my twelfth birthday. I remember that it rained constantly and that it was cold, there was nowhere to go, no one needed anything from me except for my dog, a Lab the color of earth: Edgar

was his name. I know I can go back to Deauville any-
time and lie down on the sand if I want. Edgar is dead.
I can't go back there with Edgar but I could go on my
own as soon as tomorrow morning, if I wanted: all I'd
have to do is go to the station and board a train.

ooooo

While I walk, there's something I need to tell you. I lost
my dog and my home. My lovely Edgar died, and then
my brother left to fly solo. His name is Balthazar, but
I've always called him Bal: Balthazar is just too long. We
grew up together under the same roof, and now we're
separated by the Seine. Bal has created his own little
world on rue Jacob, so we each have our separate lives.
Our parents left to go live in Buenos Aires thirty-five
days after I turned eighteen. To see them, we have to
take a twelve-hour flight—eleven with favorable winds.
Edgar is dead, and I never got another dog because I
want to remember Edgar as if he were the only dog in
the world.

I tried to shed a couple tears when my parents
left, and I failed at that, too. Our home burst like those
Pepsi bubbles on my tongue; it was the only home in
the world. Edgar was the color of dark chocolate, his
fur gleamed in the sun, he was a being capable of emotion. One day I let him try my Coke in the Compiègne

41

forest. We had been walking for several hours, we were tired, we were hungry and thirsty. I poured a couple drops on his nose, he sneezed. Edgar didn't like Coke. *Where are you, Edgar?* Edgar is dead. I walked with him on the beach at Deauville, while my brother listened to Daft Punk: they hadn't yet become mythical.

Edgar was licking my bare feet on the beach, waiting for me to throw his ball as far as I could into the ocean. He would have swum himself to death for that little green and yellow tennis ball. I lost Edgar forever, and then I lost my home: the unity dissolved! It's exceptionally hot out for this time of year; it might as well be June. I'm not in the Compiègne forest. It's almost 5:00 AM and I've finished my Pepsi.

My gaming console is broken. That's why I left the house. If it were still working, I wouldn't have had to flee; I would have let myself become absorbed by a video game instead, driving race cars, or maybe a baseball tournament. I'm not sleepy. I'm going to walk along the Tuileries and then I'm going to cross the Seine and head to rue Jacob. I want to go see my brother, to go back in time, reconnect with Balthazar—reconnect with the memory of my childhood for a handful of hours.

The different generations of Playstation have helped me take innumerable different anxieties more lightly: after the day I finished the seventh and final volume of Proust's *In Search of Lost Time*, I didn't read anything else for a year because I thought that no book could possibly live up to it, except maybe for Chateaubriand's *Memoirs from Beyond the Grave* or Nabokov's *Lolita*, but I'd already read them. So, my console is there for my mind and my solitude. I've experienced some unforgettable moments. Skiing, tennis, shooting AK-47s, parachuting, ice hockey; I've been a soldier, an athlete, a murderer, an innocent; I've won World Cups; I've roved across enormous, interminable maps, specially designed for my console and my screen: sandy deserts, fauna-lush tropical islands, icy landscapes, urban housing projects ... I, Alma, have roamed the lengths of soccer fields, basketball courts, rugby pitches. I've been to Tokyo, Palm Beach, Dubai, the Monaco Grand Prix, the 24 Hours of Le Mans ... And in those worlds, I've lived.

3

Finally, I can see the Seine. On this mild autumn night, the river is sublime, and this observation is devoid of personal sentimentalism—it's objective. Which doesn't stop me from adding that, in the end, Paris will be destroyed; the landscape before my eyes is destined to disappear. The earth will soon be deserted: this is the thought that comes to me on the Pont Neuf. But, like I've said, the world and the universe are organized to perfection: we'll soon find another planet on which to perpetuate our species—how many researchers are currently studying this question? We basically already have an answer. The earth is condemned, it's an undeniable fact. And clearly that's something to cry about, but still: nothing. The landscape that remains can't squeeze even the slightest feeling out of me. I understand this moment—I'm on the Pont Neuf, in the twenty-first century, it's 5:00 AM and the sun is eventually going to rise—but I'm detached from it, detached like my whole life is, it's all so far away from me, and I am so incapable of drawing even one moment of simple emotion into my body. Isn't that supposed to be the most important thing? Science knows it, but in the face of that word—emotion—both science and I fail. The only difference between us being that, in spite of everything, I'm capable of emotion. I've felt emotions—rarely, yes, but still I've felt them. I sat down on a bench on the bridge. I gazed at the statue of Henri IV in the distance. Its contours were fuzzy because I'm nearsighted and I refuse to wear glasses—I refuse to put a pane of glass between me and the world. So I rarely see things that are far away: I imagine them.

I could jump into the Seine—right now. I could make this day my last. I could press a knife deep into my stomach; I could disappear. And yet, sometimes it seems to me like I'm already dead. Never have I felt the end of humanity the way I did in that moment on the Pont Neuf. I wanted so badly to cry! Tears, real human tears: wet, tragic, generous! But nothing came. The world is doomed, and I can only think of one thing: drinking a Pepsi.

Look at me. You and I, all of us—we lost the cosmic game. We lost it through our excessive questions and excessive thoughts. We wanted to conquer everything that could be conquered and we failed. What does it mean to "have your reach exceed your grasp"?

It means that our senseless desire to understand drove us so far as to devour our own questions. Now nothing is left to be questioned. I think I don't know anything about being human. I'll never understand humanity, but I know the taste of Pepsi, I know its history, its colors . . . I've understood Pepsi. Who cares if this knowledge is mundane. So what if it's a trivial kind of knowledge, it's still knowledge, and we need to hold on to what we know. It's probably 5:15 AM, I'm sinking deeper into an absurd line of reasoning, but still I'm lucid, you can't even imagine how lucid. This clearheadedness probably does me more harm than good. Video games soothe my lucidity, that's why I value them so much.

I look at my shoes. They're dirty. I bought them not so long ago but haven't taken care of them. I *forgot* about my shoes. On the road, on the sidewalk, and in the park, I trudged across gravel, over concrete and cobblestones, without the slightest regard for these white canvas tennis shoes with the beat-up soles, probably spattered with undetectable amounts of canine excrement and human urine. If I lifted them to my nose (an experience I'll spare myself), I'd smell the acrid odor of rubber made in China, maybe even the faintest smell of dust from the Tuileries garden, an evocation of the *Ancien régime*.

I wonder to myself if the gas chambers smelled anything like the soles of my shoes, infinitely stronger though, naturally. I think it's possible. To know, you'd have had to ask a Jew who'd experienced the gas chambers, but all the Jews with that knowledge are dead. Would an SS officer know? According to what I've read, it seems like the SS had a remarkable gift for obedience: all it takes is an order. I would have ordered one to sniff my sneakers, I would have ordered him to tell me, on the spot, whether the smell of my shoes had any sort of link to the characteristic odor of a gas chamber after *the work was done*. You can be sure that I'd have received a positive or negative response, and with details.

I gag slightly. The brain has to be purified of all the horrors strewn throughout it, have them wiped away like traces of excrement from the sole of a shoe. I have to eliminate whatever is blocking my emotions. *I need to cry*. It's been so long. It just has to happen. I was in the drugstore on the Champs-Élysées yesterday morning and I couldn't do it. I wanted to cry at the counter, or in the book section, or in the refrigerated aisle, but all I could think about was Daft Punk and my soda, and also I thought about death, about the horror that we were forced to live out right here in Paris, not so many years ago: the mass arrests, the cattle cars full of Jews. My can of soda was cold. I enjoyed that Pepsi, it did me the biggest favor: it quenched my thirst.

ooooo

I want a better life, an extraordinary life, a life that this world as it stands cannot offer me—cannot offer anyone, for that matter. I've come to understand that I need to invent, to always be inventing, that we need to mobilize our intellectual capacities day and night: to not be reinventing the world is to die. I wish that our continent could have gotten it together, I wish the Allies had won the war in 1945. I'll say it: it's an illusion. We didn't win the war in 1945. We lost the war, and with it, control of humanity. Maybe that's why my tears will not flow.

I've cried only once in my life, I was probably in the seventh spring of my existence. I cried when, without warning, my mother ripped a Band-Aid off of my arm. I'd been wearing that Band-Aid for days, I refused to take it off, but my mother came up behind me and violently tore it off. It was unexpected, I cried out in pain and big tears, warm and salty, flowed from my almond-shaped eyes. I can picture that moment: my grandmother's apartment in Buenos Aires, my grandmother's room; I was in the middle of contemplating the watercolor illustrations in Saint-Exupéry's *The Little Prince*, the book open in my arms, my knees were bare. By soaking it with a tear, I darkened forever the Prince's planet: its warm violet moulted into a faded, linen grey.

We've lost the meaning of the word humanity; and I don't really know where I stand. I feel like the world in which I live is not a world: like, as if the time of day were constantly being tampered with, falsified. Maybe the word humanity never really meant anything. It seems to me that when it's night, it's never truly night, and when it's day, it's never truly day either. I'll say it again: the truth is we lost the war in 1945, and maybe that's why I can never tell if I'm living in a video game or not. I think I want to be in a video game, because in a video game anything is possible, all options are open, everything can be programmed into existence. To program a dream; to make it into a life—that's what I want.

∞∞∞

I looked at the sky. It was waning toward absolute darkness, but its chiaroscuro hues remained veiled with indigo; there was a hole on the horizon, paler than the midnight blue, and the clouds were like daggers moving along the ether, blocking it out, chiseling it, bringing it forth only to immediately suppress it again. I couldn't tell if the sky was dominating the clouds or if the clouds were heaven's helm—and encircled by the knives made of cloud was the cobalt-colored hole: a second world right over our heads. Maybe I ought to say a second life, since, for a moment, while contemplating this cloudscape, I had the illusion that, in that matrix above me, it might be possible to really begin anew. A spectacle of this nature could make me believe that the earth and the sky are separate from one another: that there's the earth on one hand, and the sky on the other. False: the sky belongs to this world. I've decided to reject, once and for all, the lie of divine existence. The sky is of this world, I'll say it again, and we, human beings, are alone with ourselves—a fact that I've finally accepted, and that I've even been able to rid of all its tragic connotations.

And what's more, questions bug me. Probably because of the lack of answers. Generally speaking, I ask myself no questions: I want to know as little as possible. I'll walk all the way to rue Jacob, and my brain won't be encumbered by any line of reasoning likely to lead to an interrogation. At some point in your life, if you want to do well at things, you'll need to stop asking why things are the way they are.

Children love to ask: why? and it would be dishonest of me to hide the fact that this word has caused me enormous suffering. In order to ask why, you have to be humble. I am not humble. I'm incapable of even the tiniest bit of humility. I banished the word *why* from my existence once and for all because suffering, like other feelings, needs to be diffused in reasonable quantities throughout all bodies. Suffering needs to be moderated, to remain unspectacular, or else we ruin everything. I buried the word "why" because it caused me too much suffering, and too much suffering, like too much emotion, is a waste of time. I have no time to lose (if in fact

I haven't already irremediably wasted all of my time) because this world is blazing, and I need to be up to the challenge of that adjective if I want to be able to live. I want that—to live—though it doesn't belong to the order of desire. It's a duty we must carry out. We are born, and consequently we must live. I'll never venture any further down this line of reasoning. I told you already that I refuse to question, I settle for following the course of things: nothing interests me other than the way things unfold. That being said, I sometimes find myself falling back into old habits. Succumbing to the why. But it doesn't happen often: I try to obey the event itself. Sentences materialize in our thinking, we don't choose their form, and thought, after all, is a mysterious enclave. I made the choice to trust in my thinking, just as I trust my memory (as errant as it may well be) because I have nothing else—and that's a strong enough argument to sway me.

I wait to see what's going to happen, that's what I meant by "I obey the event itself." I am open to the present state of things. The why, I feel no necessity to know. I want to be there when these things happen. I want to be able to hold my can of Pepsi, and let my memory replay years of Pepsi ads inside my brain, without asking myself why. I have the strange impression this night will never end.

ooooo

I'm not thinking about the time, it doesn't matter anymore. I've hit a point in the night where time and place have been stripped of all concrete and valid meaning. It makes me think of December 1941: the month when humanity lost all concrete and valid meaning. December 1941 was an important historical moment: it was the month that the plan to exterminate the entire Jewish population of Europe was put into action. The plan that would determine my grandfather's life. In December 1941, Himmler and Hitler decided that my grandfather needed to disappear. The verb *disparaître*, to disappear, is nebulous. The German verb for disappearance is *aussterben*. The significance of *sterben* is clear: it means to die. But the *aus* is more complex—to disappear doesn't necessarily mean to die. As far as I'm concerned, I've often thought of disappearance as an opportunity. In a world where the map precedes the territory, to disappear from the map is to abandon yourself to something like an adventure. Sometimes, I want to experience adventure: yes, sometimes I do, in fact, want to disappear. December 1941 is nothing other than the setting in motion of the plan to make an entire race disappear. What I want to know, first of all, is if Hitler, Heydrich, Himmler and Eichmann reflected on the verb *aussterben*, even for a moment: I want to know if Hitler, Heydrich,

Himmler and Eichmann were aware of the multiple meanings of the German verb *aussterben*, to know if they were familiar with its French equivalent, *disparaître*. Because it would be good for those who are executing the final solution, or otherwise said, the disappearance of a people in its entirety, to know what the word *disappear* means. Hitler failed. Heydrich failed. Himmler failed. Eichmann failed. The disappearance was not total—the proof being that I, myself, am on the Pont Neuf formulating this sentence. What has not disappeared in its entirety cannot be said to have disappeared at all. Disappearance cannot be partial: that's a misconception. And admitting this poses an enormous problem for certain individuals. Namely, if Hitler, Heydrich, Himmler and Eichmann did not succeed in making all the Jews of Europe disappear, it must mean that they did not succeed in making any Jews disappear. It is extremely late at night and this argument astonishes me, yet all I can do is confirm that it's self-evident. Hitler, Heydrich, Himmler, and Eichmann 100 percent failed, which should be enough to make them roll over in their graves, wherever they are, even if they're only dust, even if they never had graves. And if my reasoning is sound for the Jews, I have to admit, reluctantly, that it must also be true for Nazis. The Nazis have not entirely disappeared, which amounts to saying that none of them have disappeared.

Hitler, Heydrich, Himmler, and Eichmann are still with us, the poison and the hanging are powerless to change that. I could just as well say: we're still in December 1941, and a part of Europe is readying itself to be partially destroyed. I told you a little while ago that truth is not a matter of facts, but it's a fact, too, that time is not a matter of clocks. Even less so in this time, my time, when I can't even keep the days straight. It didn't take reading *Memoirs from Beyond the Grave* or *In Search of Lost Time* for me to grasp this phenomenon. The perpetual shiftings of my memory were enough to take me by surprise, to make me see that time returns ceaselessly, to the point that I don't know who I am—which is probably lucky since I've always struggled to believe in that thing called identity. But when time returns, it returns with the same balance of life and death. In the face of these difficulties, I am powerless.

I have only the event. And in the face of the event, there's nothing to be done but be there. I like being there: saying nothing. Letting my thoughts and my body accept that Hitler, Heydrich, Himmler and Eichmann will never disappear. That Jews will never disappear. That the can I hold in my hand is blue and red, that it reminds me of visual sensations linked to TV. I've accepted all of it, and I want to add that I've never seen death in a negative way, or as a kind of punishment. Death is what we are. It's in the landscape; in the extravagant sky that towers above me, and which seems to be growing lighter and lighter, but maybe my longing for dawn is corrupting my perception. Death is in the can I've just drained; it is everywhere in my memory—past, present, to come. I'm going to go all the way to rue Jacob and I'm going to hold my brother in my arms. Maybe there'll be some Coke in his fridge. I'll tell him I'm thirsty. I'll suggest that we play a video game together, waiting for the café down the street to open its doors so that we can feast on *tartines* and croissants. I'm not hungry yet, but by 7:00 AM I'll be famished. Some things are possible to predict, hunger is one of them—barring the possibility that an anxiety-induced nausea could surge up and hinder my cerebral functioning. Because the question of hunger is not posed by the stomach: it comes from the brain. Hunger is, before all else, something intellectual. Now that I think about it, a stomach never directly cries out that it's famished. What I'm saying is probably not 100 percent scientifically accurate, but walking along rue Guénégaud, not thinking about anything seems to me a choice made out of extreme sadness. It's not that the street is sad, it's a pretty street, but also a hopeless one. A street very much like me, deep down. It's been a few years since I did away with hope for good, but actually, having said that—maybe I never had any to begin with.

4

I take rue de Seine, the wind that blows here has a unique smell: it carries with it the freshness of a distant sea, algae, and maybe also the sum of all the body parts decaying at the bottom of the river, prisoners of the mud. The bodies of animals, cats, dogs, maybe even horses—and then, of course, human bodies.

Soon I'll be at Balthazar's, we'll play video games. Those who claim that life is complicated are wrong: life is not complicated. All you need to do is walk half an hour a day, eat a little, work a little, sleep a little, drink 1.5 liters of non-alcoholic liquid every twenty-four hours. What's complicated is wanting to be successful and not succeeding. I said earlier that I wanted to leave and never go home. I think, though, that I lied. I gave up on the word success a while ago now. To tell the truth, I gave up on it precisely because I came to the conclusion that life is not complicated. And to those of us who think that life isn't complicated, the word success no longer elicits strong emotions. The verb to succeed no longer manages to agitate me—that's definitely something new, and it comes with its own brand of horror. I'm going to see Bal soon, we'll play on his console, and then we'll stuff ourselves with butter croissants in some bistro while the day finally establishes itself. I'll try to remember some of what Hume says about causality while Bal consults the most recent barrage of emails on his tablet. We'll say goodbye in a simple way, there'll be a kind of ease, that discreet reserve which exists only between those who share the same blood, and who also shared a childhood, with its bunk beds, toys, wagers, and baths.

I'd like to repeat that I'm not afraid to die, but it has literally nothing to do with the question at hand. That question is: what do I do if Balthazar doesn't let me in? I think: maybe he's just gotten back from a night out, he can't sleep, and so he's watching TV and snacking. A Kubrick film or an animal documentary—at 5:00 AM, anything does the trick. I remember that we would sit on the rug in the living room, hands submerged in a bowl of popcorn. I would reach my whole hand in, but only ever chose one kernel at a time, while Balthazar would suddenly grab the bowl to bring it closer, accusing me of taking all the sweet stuff. My brother has always been skinny, in spite of the fact that, for a long time, he consumed alarming quantities of sugar. The popcorn didn't even register in our field of vision, it had no real existence for us, it wasn't there to accompany whatever was playing on our screens, or even to satisfy a craving. We were focused on the TV or the computer, watching moments burst forth out of nothingness. I swam through the screen-world, and it was like living a second time. Face to face with the screens, I had no age. I didn't know what I was watching, but it wasn't just images: each one was a moment detached from all other moments. The screens were an inexhaustible source of pink, bright red, turquoise, pure white, yellow, gray, but never black. It was a sea— no, even more vast: it was an ocean of ever-renewing colors. On Wednesdays, Bal and I would let ourselves be swept inside that cavern of texture and sound, like the hollow place created by a wave as it breaks. We were spellbound—that's exactly the right word for it. Everything was ceaselessly starting over, there was no continuity to those moments, no common thread running through them, as if time were no longer at work, at least not in that room, not in the TV or the computer, and maybe that was the kind of time that I internalized. It's possible that I'm going to Balthazar's now, not knowing what time it is, not knowing if he's even going to let me in, because I grew up surrounded by screens, and that means that all this doesn't mean the same thing to me as it would to someone who learned time from clocks. My relationship with time is nothing but an enormous knot of chaos.

It's possible to think that screens destroyed me, but that would be a misconception. Screens didn't destroy me, they just offered me a different relationship to the world. By "world," I mostly mean a different relationship to time, because if you subtract time, what remains of "the world"? If it so happens that Bal doesn't open the door, if he doesn't let me in because he's sleeping, I'll wait on the landing, eventually I'll even fall asleep on the stairs, head lolled back against the old wrought-iron railing. His stairwell is always cold, like most stairwells. It's dusty, too, and electrical wires hang down parallel to the door frames. Traces of mildew have appeared along the top edges of the already damaged walls, covered in forty-year-old paint that is peeling into innumerable little shards. If I think about it, Bal's building is borderline unsanitary, it's derelict, which surprises me a bit considering its economic and geographical position in the city. But isn't that just what everyone is looking for: contrast? Dirty things at the heart of clean things, clean things at the heart of dirty things; ugly things that contain something beautiful, beautiful things that conceal hideousness. No, there's no way that Bal won't let me in because I'll knock loud enough that, worst case scenario, I'll give him an unpleasant wake up. It'll definitely put him in a bad mood, but that doesn't matter, because a brother who doesn't ever get annoyed isn't really a brother.

ooooo

I stopped in front of number 12 rue Jacob; the door was already open so I didn't have to use the intercom. I entered the lobby, took the stairs right up to the fourth floor and, without even thinking, laughing to hide my apprehension, I knocked on the door three times. I glanced to the right and saw a doorbell. I didn't remember Bal having a doorbell, I'd never seen it before. Funny, how such important details are capable of secretly self-destructing in our memory—as to why this happens, I'm in no state to answer. I could have rung the doorbell, but having just pounded on the green door with my fist, the doorbell route had already been foreclosed to me, since I know that knocking and then ringing is impolite and excessive. I'm not an outwardly inappropriate person: I wear my eccentricities on the inside. I act with moderation in mind. I abstain from using the doorbell.

No one answers. While I wait, I empty my mind, aiming for a complete emptiness, the emptiness of waiting, but it doesn't work and my brain fills right back up again, firing on all cylinders, so to control myself, I begin to count. At first I count to thirty, and when that doesn't help I count to sixty, because sixty seconds equals one minute, and one minute is a whole little world. I feel disappointment stealing across my face, as though a wave of darkness were washing over me, gnawing at me like a little rat gnaws at a piece of meat. So I ring. For the first time in my life, I use that doorbell. It's an old doorbell, old-fashioned, the kind whose ring reverberates through the silence of the night and of my own abandonment. I'm still counting. But little by little, I begin to give up. I call Balthazar several times, his voice-mail continually slamming the door in my hopeful face. I just let it go, the way you suddenly let go of something long desired, let it fall from your life without giving it any real thought: moved by purest indifference.

I knew it wasn't too important but it made me sad anyway

I said that I've never tried to understand. And it's this kind of situation that only reaffirms that choice to me, to never seek to understand anything in this world. I found myself on the sidewalk on rue Jacob, in front of my brother's building, and I wondered if we'd ever really been friends, he and I, beyond being linked by blood. This was an idiotic thought, and yet it presented itself seriously to my mind. Not all my thoughts deserve to see the light of day; I contain my own percentage of atrocity and insignificance, like empty husks or scraps

of thoughts, held in that gray matter, in what consti-
tutes my relation to all that I see, all that I am (if I am
something). To tell you that I'm this or that would just
be lying to you, spitting in your face: I'll never formulate
it that way, I'll never say what I am. Then "One More
Time" immediately popped back into my head, along
with some naked bodies, heaped on top of each other
in a gas chamber, just as I'd imagined them earlier. I
made the mistake of listening to Daft Punk just after
that image had become fixed in my mind—I hope that
the two will not remain permanently linked; unless I
were to try to identify some aesthetic dimension in this
association between Auschwitz and Daft Punk: that's
an odious thought.

Our faith in the future is doled out in meager quantities

I went downstairs. I stared at the intercom for a long
time. My brother's initials weren't there. *BF* was nowhere
to be found: *BF* did not exist. I thought that someone
must have ripped them off. I touched the intercom, I
lingered over some of the initials inscribed on its labels,
and quickly, I scraped them off to see if someone had
taped over my brother's initials.

I tore off three stickers, and under the third one I
found Bal's initials hidden by a label that had no writing on it at all. I put the blank one in my pocket and

left my brother's initials to reoccupy their rightful place.
I pressed on the little black button beside Bal's initials,
checking once more to see whether he was there, just
in case he might have been sleeping and hadn't heard
my knocking, or the doorbell I'd rung for the first time.
I tried three times, waiting sixty seconds between each
attempt, counting sheep. Nothing. It was definitive: I'd
lost, again, like always—losing is an integral part of my
life. I'm hungry now and I don't want to eat alone. I am
hit with a sudden craving for a powdered donut, like
before.

Everything is possible

I walk along rue Jacob, determined but shaky: a waver-
ing blade of grass. I focus on imagining the aesthetic
qualities of a donut. A voice inside me says: *He lives
in Los Angeles.* I'd rather die of hunger than eat alone.
It's my own voice, it addresses me, it's repeating softly,
warmly: *He lives in Los Angeles.* I think I don't have any
real limits anymore because I no longer have any real
desires, I can probably make it through whatever happens because I don't want any of what's offered to me,
here, in this life, other than food and drink. But food
and drink don't elicit any kind of emotion from me, and
what I'm searching for this morning is to feel something, any emotion, no matter how small. I don't know

if the pursuit of feeling counts as a desire; I don't think so. It's not that I desire emotion, it's just something that I'm seeking. There is no link between the act of searching and desire, this proposition seems acceptable to me. And yet, on occasion, while standing in front of a display filled with donuts, I've felt something. I remember the shiver I felt the first time I went into the American chain, Dunkin Donuts. It was just after buying a new stuffed animal from FAO Schwartz, on Fifth Avenue in New York. The floor tiling was an undefinable color, maybe gray but luminous still, after all the years of wear; the dense smell of cold grease and ground coffee, and, behind the counter, displayed—exposed, even—in a thoughtful way, as if it were an art installation: dozens of donuts enrobed in the most outrageous, powerful, charismatic colors. Cotton-candy pink, cream, yellow, green, red, turquoise, purple: fluorescent or dark, some topped with multicolored sprinkles. I don't know how old I was, but I remember thinking: *I'll never have to be hungry again.* I think that abundance moved me. There are few things in this life that you can choose. At Dunkin Donuts, you could choose the color, the flavor, the amount. You could decide if you wanted sprinkles or not (I always wanted sprinkles). Their donuts were available all day and all night—24/7—I didn't have to think about death, I no longer had to be afraid, alone in my bed at night, because while I slept, this place was open, and it had donuts—we've never heard of a Dunkin Donuts running out of donuts, logically speaking, it's unlikely. This image of abundance and that moment of realization have remained engraved in my memory. So really, I should congratulate everyone who created and participated in the design and the execution of such a brilliant idea—once again, I have to bow my head in admiration. I'm often tempted to ask: *Just how far is it possible to go?* But since that counts as a question, I restrain myself.

∞∞∞

I don't know how much I actually want a donut: if it's a real desire or an illusion. I put on my headphones and I sit on the sidewalk, back against the window of a store selling chairs on rue Saint-Benoît. I'm there, in the peacefulness of dawn, lulled by Daft Punk's soft and measured robot voices. A dog has definitely peed on the spot where I'm sitting, but since dogs are generally more worthy than humans—I'd say, more loyal—I've decided to accept the possibility that I'm getting particles of dog urine on my jeans. Still, a shiver ripples through me. It's also possible that the hypothetical traces of urine came from a homeless person, or some haggard young man caught short coming out of the Montana hotel. I give up on weighing the pros and cons, I get up, thinking to myself that I'll never wear these jeans again. But I know I'm lying. I'll wear them again. They just need to be washed. I dig around in my pockets. I don't have my credit card, the world's most enjoyed form of payment. I've got eleven euros and thirty cents: a bill, three coins. I don't think I need any more. Probably because it's Sunday.

There was no life so there was no emotion

I notice that rue Saint-Benoît has no trees. Neither does rue Jacob. I'm reminded of a documentary I saw last week about the deportation of Jewish children from Paris to Bergen-Belsen. Her name was Denise Bimbad, I won't forget her name; she said that walking through Bergen-Belsen among the bodies that littered the ground was like passing by clusters of trees. She said: "There was no life so there was no emotion." It was just part of the scenery. To her—a child—life was movement. No movement meant no emotion. In my eyes, a tree contains a certain emotional potential. I wouldn't go so far as to say that every tree moves me, but rather that each one opens the possibility of being moved. Denise Bimbad didn't see bodies, she saw trees and she felt nothing. But then, she felt nothing because she wasn't really seeing trees, either. She didn't see trees like she didn't see bodies. Denise Bimbad saw bodies imitating trees: what she saw was a thousand bodies imitating a forest. I remember precisely that I turned off the TV, threw the remote on the ground, and ate a purple popsicle that had been in the back of my freezer for months. I thought about the blood of dead people, of what happens to the blood inside a corpse. It dries up. Then I went to bed. I slept admirably well that night, long and deep—for me, that's a rare thing, I think I even dreamed of trees, possibly a forest. Sometimes I dream of the Compiègne forest, and often Edgar comes to walk beside me in my dreams. He barks in the heart of the empty forest, the ground perforated by enormous trees, a forest with no geographical limit, an unending landscape, a real dreamscape. Edgar barks for me to throw his ball.

∞∞∞∞

I don't know what time it is anymore; I've lost all notion of time. I don't know if I'll see the sun again someday. Sometimes, we realize we no longer know anything. It reminds us that we never really knew anything in the first place, that we'll never know anything—I use the first person plural here, but, to be clear, I'm speaking in my own name.

This morning, it seems to me that I've already lost. But if I dig a little deeper, I can see I made a mistake believing that it was ever a game I could win. I'm not in a video game. I'm not in Mario Kart. After all, I don't know what the verb "to die" means, I'll experience it as I'm ejected from my body; meaning, more precisely, my body will experience—not me. In video games, after *game over*, we can come back. In truth, we'll never lose, we exist in the very impossibility of losing: we play again. It's possible that it's the same in this world, but that's a theory no one can confirm. Maybe I'm destined to eternally relive, like in a game, that thing people call "life" (or "the world," in the end it's the same thing). Reliving eternally, at other points in time, in space, in another body, in a completely different configuration: to be destined to begin life again. In a word: to be surrounded.

ooooo

My grandfather's name was Jacob. That's something I could have revealed when I first arrived at my brother's building, standing there on rue Jacob, but the coincidence is just so powerful—that Balthazar should live on the only street in Paris which bears our grandfather's name—it almost seemed vulgar to open with it. So I kept the connection quiet; I kept silent about Jacob, but just because I didn't mention it doesn't mean it wasn't on my mind.

It's a painful ordeal for me to enter into language,

especially when that language faces outward. Choices need to be made about what I give and what I keep. There are some things we could have kept to ourselves. There are even sentences we might have preferred not to even think, not to see the light of day even in our own minds. Sentences we should have been able to eradicate simply, like vermin. And because of this fact, I regularly feel the need to sidestep speech, to avoid it for a while, even if I fail with predictable regularity in the execution . . . There are days when I tell myself I could fall into silence and remain there until my dying day. It's a worthy objective, to remain silent: it belongs to the order of illusion.

∞∞∞

I continue on my way. I know where I'm going. The metro isn't open yet, there might be one last night bus, but I don't care. I'm not really tired, or maybe it's a tiredness so intense that I don't feel it anymore, it's mutated into a feeling of being electrified—like when it's so cold that you start to feel warm, or when freezing water runs over your fingers and burns them.

I feel good when I'm walking, I feel like I think better, like my thoughts are generally more coherent: my brain gets into a flow. The movement of my feet is in sync with the movement of my thoughts. They're constantly hungry—my thoughts—they eat away at me. I could call them my ants, my blow flies, my leeches, except instead of my blood, they're gnawing at my brain and my mood, and maybe also my innocence and my faith in God, too—they ruin everything.

I could say that my thoughts work like a Swiss watch. There's no knobs or buttons, nothing to wind manually; no battery to change—they run ceaselessly, they feed on themselves, all they need is my breath, my being alive: movement. I felt weary and I turned off Daft Punk. I stashed my headphones in the pocket of my jeans. I'm listening to the silence of Paris. You can hear the birds; there are almost no cars at all. I'm getting closer to the Seine: I'll follow it west.

II

Adolf Hitler checkmated humanity.

1

Sometimes events destabilize us. I don't believe in signs, and yet there are certain events that should push me to start. I haven't said anything—I wanted to silence that absurd encounter—but now it seems to me I can't hide it any longer.

It was a little less than thirty-six hours ago. It was Friday evening, the moon was shining. I had dinner plans with a cousin visiting from Buenos Aires. I was feeling relaxed. I was having a good day—full of light and tranquility.

I said this already: sometimes things collapse inside us and in front of us; our lives come undone. The cause isn't always something extraordinary—it can be, though. It's all a matter of perspective, everything is a question of distance.

I went into a restaurant on rue Oberkampf. And in that moment, my life flickered slightly. I say "slightly" because I don't believe in ruptures. At least—I don't want to.

By the time I got there, she was already seated. She was blond as a wheat field. She had walnut-colored eyes. It wasn't her face that shook me: it was her name. I kissed my cousin, and then my cousin said to me: "This is Martha Eichmann." The name blinded me: some names call out to us. The name Eichmann I recognized.

"THIS IS MARTHA EICHMANN"

She looked like her grandfather. The same fox-like features. Stretched face, roman nose, half pinched mouth which constrained all its utterances. I saw a montage of History unfold across a face. I saw the number 6,000,000. I saw Adolf Hitler's suicide. I saw Claus von Stauffenberg's failure. I saw death. I saw abandonment. I saw the lack of love. I didn't shake her hand, I kissed her on both cheeks. I didn't feel any kind of emotion. No nausea. I was no longer in the world; I was in another dimension. I could have been angry with my cousin, I could have said: *Why did you betray us?* But to say such a thing would never have occurred to me. If I follow the reasoning of our time, Martha Eichmann and Adolf Eichmann are two separate beings. Martha has nothing to do with her grandfather: Martha is a free and innocent individual.

Same face

I wasn't hungry, I forced myself. I ate red meat. It was almost raw. I lost the notion of time, I forgot my own name, I forgot everything. I'll say it: during the time I ate my meat (maybe ten minutes) my memory was shut off. I stepped out of the river of History. I was suspended in a reality without relations. I was watching Martha Eichmann eat her meat, I was watching her chew the dead animal, making sure to smile at her.

We talked about her grandfather. My cousin seemed to be enjoying asking her questions. He intended to circumvent all uneasiness: not talking about it was worse than talking about it. We talked about Auschwitz.

I had to remind her of the name of the camp

Martha Eichmann couldn't remember the name of the camp. I had to remind her of the name of the camp: I had to help her. She was searching for the word. I said: "Auschwitz?" Martha Eichmann answered: "Yes, that's it—Auschwitz." She spoke Spanish like a country girl. There was something touching about her intonations. Auschwitz said nothing to her: Auschwitz did not *speak* to her. Martha was elsewhere.

Some names are hard to bear. Sometimes we have only one choice: forget our name. Martha Eichmann and I have one thing in common: we each want to forget a piece of what came before us, the difference being that Martha Eichmann has perfectly succeeded. You would have seen it in her eyes: they testified to the success of forgetting. I couldn't finish the meat I ordered: Martha Eichmann was able to finish hers. Beings react differently to their pasts. There are those who succeed; there are those who fail. I am regularly pulled under by what came before me. That night, Martha Eichmann wasn't pulled under by what came before her. I can choose to believe in destinies. Or I can choose not to.

A trickle of blood ran across my plate. I should have thought of the dead. I didn't think of the dead. The tablecloth was soft, 100 percent cotton. My hands slid over it: I was searching for whiteness. I looked at Martha Eichmann, then I looked elsewhere, then I looked at Martha Eichmann again. I kept saying to myself: "Alma, you're not in a video game here."

If I'd thrown up my steak, I'd have puked cow's blood, but I didn't. I felt calm, I went home. I was drunk (not drunk on alcohol, drunk on something else—it's impossible to explain). I spoke to my grandfather in the obscurity of my room. I said to him: "Grandfather, I had dinner with Eichmann's granddaughter!" I was enthusiastic; I would even say: exultant. He didn't answer me. I could have insulted his silence; I didn't insult his silence. I went to bed but I didn't sleep. I got up and pulled on a pair of shorts. I left my house again. I walked for five minutes through the deserted streets. I had a moment of weariness, an impression that there was nowhere to go. I went back up to my room. I was thirsty, not thirsty for Coke—thirsty for beauty. My video-game console wasn't working. I wanted to read some Malcolm Lowry poems so I opened the book. The title of the poem I opened to at random was "Thoughts to be erased from my destiny"—you can choose not to believe me: sometimes coincidences are provocative.

§

It's possible Friday evening marks the moment I began to drift off course. Or I've been drifting for years now without really knowing it. Regardless, when I got back to my room Friday night, I thought: *I am adrift.* It was the first time I'd ever had a thought like that. Before, I was living in ignorance. We can, for the most part, choose to open or close our eyes to the world. I think on Friday night I opened them. Now I want to close them. That's why I'm going to see the steeplechase and why I'm walking along the Seine. I'll be there soon, probably one kilometer left, one and a half at most.

How can I have thought so badly of the world when help has been within my reach all along?

I closed the collection of poems. Where was my help? That's when I went outside. It was nice out, the temperature was crisp but sweet. Malcolm Lowry died torn apart: toward the end, he stopped shaving and started drinking his cologne. Even Malcolm Lowry wasn't able to conquer it all in the end; he burrowed deeper into misery and solitude. I don't know what my end will be like, if I'll end up torn apart like Lowry. Ideally, I'd like to end my days in the country, in a house full of grace and silence. Maybe on the shore of a lake or at the edge of a forest. I don't know if we get to choose our own future—if we're able to decide to lose, and tunnel deeper into self-destruction; or otherwise to "turn toward the light," as they say. I don't want to die like Malcolm Lowry. Truthfully, I don't want to die at all.

The idea of softness intrigues me. I don't know if I'm a gentle person. I only believe I'm someone capable of softness. It's like asking the question: is Mahler's music gentle? Who knows? Mahler is sometimes soft, sometimes hard, torn, bitter, light, tragic. Were the Nazis capable of gentleness? Malcolm Lowry died June 26, 1957, with his wife, alcohol, and barbiturates at his side. I can't tell you if Adolf Hitler drank alcohol before dying. I still don't know if he died gently: softness is a kind of love. Adolf Hitler was not capable of love, or else he would have spared his wife. That is, unless Adolf Hitler had understood that the world to come would be void of hope.

My whole life, every time I've won a game, I've felt something like a lightning bolt inside me. A euphoria burning inside me, right to my heart. It doesn't last long, maybe a couple seconds or a couple minutes, and then the euphoria inverts. There's a kind of disappointment. I'm tempted to ask myself why nothing lasts. Obviously, I won't. Winning belongs to the realm of illusion, but losing doesn't. For example: it belongs to the realm of illusion to believe I'll live forever, but thinking that one day I'll disappear does not.

It has to be 7:00 AM now, I look at the sky. It's almost a trenchcoat-beige. I should have told Martha Eichmann her grandfather failed, that he didn't succeed in eliminating all the Jews of Europe. He must have known it. And yet, when I looked at Martha Eichmann, I thought I saw the illusion of victory in her eyes. When I uttered the name Adolf Eichmann in her presence, I sensed a hint of respect, even a certain pride. After all, Adolf Eichmann wasn't just anyone. Adolf Eichmann was someone, just like Hitler was someone: it is through evil deeds that their names entered History, and by evil deeds that they distinguished themselves. Their destinies are forever linked to the memory of men, something of them is immortal—that's a form of victory.

To certain people, winning is all that matters. But it's true, I'll repeat it: Adolf Eichmann didn't go all the

way, because if he had—if Adolf Eichmann had eradicated the Jewish people in its entirety—I could not
have found myself, on Friday evening, seated at a table
in the company of Martha Eichmann, his granddaughter: I wouldn't have existed. I would've liked to explain
to Martha Eichmann that our presence, on that evening, at that table, in that restaurant on rue Oberkampf,
was proof of her grandfather's failure, but I didn't have
the courage. I was afraid of her reaction; I didn't want to
risk her leaving the table, since Martha Eichmann too
belongs to History: she's a trace. You don't chase off a
trace—you observe it for as long as possible, and then
watch it perish.

§

As I observed Martha Eichmann, I asked myself
whether she wasn't already dead, immured by the trace
her grandfather left in the world, the same trace that his
name has transmitted to her. Sometimes I ask myself
the same question: have I been entombed by the trace
left on me by my ancestors? Traces can bury us alive.
That's why I want to forget. To be buried is to be unable
to live; I want to be able to live. There are traces which
flatter our pride, others which reassure us, still others
which disturb and frighten us. To feel attached to something—to a story, a name, a genealogy, a being, a family

... that matters. A trace can wound too—I feel wounded by certain traces. Friday night, Martha Eichmann twisted the knife in my wound. The knife: her name, her ignorance, her invisible sense of triumph.

To escape the trace

On May 31, 1962, Israeli prison guard Shalom Nagar pulled a handle which set the gallows in motion. Two minutes before midnight, the trapdoor opened beneath the engineer of the camps. The grandfather of Martha Eichmann fell into the void with his slippers on his feet. He refused a blindfold: he wanted to see death. His last wish was a glass of wine from Carmel. Among the last words of Adolf Eichmann were "Long Live Germany," which makes me think of the last words of Claus von Stauffenberg: "Long Live Sacred Germany." The dead face of Adolf Eichmann was swollen and colorless. It was the first time Shalom Nagar had seen a hanged man. On him too there is a trace—like a spot. We come into contact with individuals and those individuals come undone, shedding some small part of themselves on us. Even an infinitesimal part is a part all the same. Shalom Nagar will never forget the name: Adolf Eichmann. Nor will his children. Nor will Martha Eichmann. Nor will I. Nor will History. Nor will our world. The names that have done evil enter our memory in just as intense a way as the names that have done good. We establish no hierarchy. The name Hitler isn't far from being as famous as the name Jesus Christ, or the name Michael Jackson. We throw all History's names into a big bag and mix them up. Sometimes, I ask myself if we're still in a position to distinguish between the good names and the bad, if we really make a distinction at all. There's a kind of indifference. I think in today's world, Hitler is a myth in the same way Jesus Christ is a myth and Michael Jackson is a myth: we can't forget these names because they've put down roots in our memories. The 14,000,000 human beings exterminated between 1933 and 1945 aren't myths: we don't know their names. They are dust. They are numbers. Whether that's just or not isn't the question. Morality is like the fact of winning: it's an illusion.

Look at what we've done. We made the victims into a cluster of numbers, and then we turned the executioners into a tangle of myths.

2

Day arrives before my very eyes—a timid sun nibbling at the moon. And I follow the river as my memory delves into its own contents. In my head, I begin thousands of different thoughts, but only finish a few of them: finishing things is harder than starting them. One day, this world began, and one day, it will have to be interrupted. Sometimes, I feel so afraid of an ending, of something ending, that I rush to bring it about. Maybe it's the same with our world: we are so afraid of it ending that we hasten its collapse. What will remain of this world when the human beings who populated it have been annihilated?

I said earlier that we'll soon find another planet where we can perpetuate our species, but I think that might be yet another illusion. We will end with the Earth: when she disintegrates, we will disintegrate with her. I don't think there's any reason to cry, and even less to feel regret.

Where lies the beginning, there too lies the end

I wonder what my final thought will end up being: maybe my final thought will be empty. Like the final thoughts of the dead exterminated on the edge of a pit, a bullet in the back of the head. I don't know if my final thought will be one of hatred or of love. I don't know if I'll see colors. I want to be able to control the world; I'll never control the world.

I could have kept my thoughts quiet. I could have censored them until the day of my death. I accepted that I was going to die: fear of death can't be the cause, at least, not any more than my taste for scandalizing. Who's pushing me to the edge of the ravine? Who's pushing me to open myself in such a dangerous way? I've kept everything inside, I've built up a reserve of recollections. Everything is there in my memory, I don't think I left anything behind. It overflows, then drains out, then overflows again, like the movement of waves on a beach. I preserved even the most insignificant moments: from one of my brother's underhanded jokes to an interminable all-nighter; from a little ray of sunlight to the death of my dog.

Heroes don't exist

Claus von Stauffenberg was eliminated on July 21, 1944,

a little before one o'clock in the morning. I said that his last words were: "Long Live Sacred Germany." I don't know what is hidden behind that expression. Probably yet another illusion. We accumulate a store of innumerable beliefs. Claus von Stauffenberg is not a hero by any measure. He failed twice over. The Valkyrie operation that was supposed to kill Hitler fell like a drop in the ocean. By July 20, 1944, several million Jews were already dead—not to mention the others. Claus von Stauffenberg was not ahead of his time, in fact he wasn't even on time to meet it: Claus von Stauffenberg was scandalously late. Wanting to kill Hitler on July 20, 1944 is like wanting to start living when you're already on your deathbed: even if he had succeeded, it would have still been completely pointless. Nevertheless, we should acknowledge that he is one of the only ones who ever dared to try.

I LIVE IN A WORLD THAT WAS NOT ABLE TO ERADICATE ADOLF HITLER

On April 30, around 3:30 PM, when the Red Army is no more than a few hundred meters away from the bunker, Adolf Hitler commits suicide alongside Eva Braun. Hitler commits suicide by shooting himself in the mouth.

Adolf Hitler decided the moment of his death. We

allowed him to commit suicide; we thus allowed him to win the game: checkmate. Adolf Hitler isn't dead, he hasn't even disappeared. If the Allies had taken him out, Adolf Hitler might have disappeared. But his suicide turns History upside down.

The suicide of Adolf Hitler is no detail: it is of the highest importance. Committing suicide is not dying. Committing suicide is not disappearing. To commit suicide is to bring about a short-circuit. Adolf Hitler knew that, that's the reason he shot himself in the mouth. Maybe if the Allies had killed Adolf Hitler, we would have won in 1945. If Claus von Stauffenberg's attack had succeeded, then we could have won the war.

We lost the Second World War because of a suicide

I just said it, and I'll say it again: we had the illusion of victory in 1945, while in reality, we failed. I'm not saying that the Nazis won the war: I'm saying that Adolf Hitler won it with his suicide, and you should trust me on this. We are still living with the short-circuit set off by one man, alone.

It's obvious that if Hitler had never existed, the world as it is today would not be the same. I won't venture to say whether it would have been better—or worse—I'm only saying that Hitler's birth, as well as his suicide, set the terms for the time in which we live.

Continuing on in the same world after Adolf Hitler's short-circuit was simply not possible: firstly, it was too humiliating. Above all, it was illogical: Adolf Hitler turned the human species into a species of rat; he compromised the meaning of the word *humanity*. We thus found ourselves obligated to design a new world, one where the word *humanity* has a new meaning. This new world has its own conventions and its own history: in the new world, we won the war in 1945. The remaking of History is not just a possibility: it is often a necessity.

Why are we so attached to the virtual? I could pose this question to each one of us. It's impossible to deny the validity of this statement: The virtual has invaded our era. I don't know if that's a coincidence: to tell the truth, I don't think so. After April 30, 1945, we gradually sank deeper and deeper into the technology of screens. It wasn't a choice, it was a spiral: we needed to forget that defeat, forget the wound inflicted on humanity. So we quickly configured a planet almost completely submerged in the virtual, because it's just a fact that screens wipe our memories clean. To forget, that's our perennial need, it's what I want, and the time in which I live has a talent for forgetting—for that, I appreciate it, in the most innocent and pure way. The virtual makes me forget the worst, namely: Hitler's triumph.

Screens try by all possible means to destroy

whatever remains of my memory. When I'm on my Mac, when I'm in front of my TV, when I'm playing video games, I no longer know where I am or what day it is, my brain is empty, my brain is washed clean: I leave behind my memory, leave time, I step out of the river of History. We shouldn't turn away from the things that do us good. It's not coincidental that our world puts all its faith in the virtual: it's our only hope of forgetting.

This is only a hypothesis, but I believe it right now: it's possible that the origin of the existence of my Mac, my video games—of all technology—lies in the occurrence of both Adolf Hitler's suicide and Claus von Stauffenberg's failed assassination attempt. Adolf Hitler committed suicide with a woman born the same year as my grandfather, in 1912. We can choose to turn away from coincidences or we can choose to face them: I've chosen to open my eyes to the coincidences. I don't know, though, in any event, whether it's possible to speak in terms of a choice. It might be more like a curse. The more we link events to one another, the more we lose our innocence. Innocence makes it possible to live in peace with the world, in a certain way—I said before that, for me, the world is another word for time. I am not at peace with time. I'm not at peace with the world. And it's not for lack of desire: I want to be at peace with all of you. Maybe someday I'll manage it. Maybe I won't. Who decides? I don't know. Ever since

I eliminated God from my life, I no longer know anything. Knowing nothing comes with risks. It's living on the edge of an abyss. I do want to know; I do want to believe in God. But God, too, failed in the face of my illusion: God doesn't act upon this world. That's why I'm so angry with him. Sure, being angry with God is useless, but it's a fact that most of the feelings we experience during our existence are useless. I'll add: we ourselves are completely superfluous. And maybe that's our opportunity, our chance. This thought came to me, I could have suppressed it, locked it away somewhere deep and dark, but instead I decided to open myself to it. Hitler probably dreamed of usefulness: that his actions would serve his destiny, as well as that of the German nation.

Adolf Hitler is one of the most important names in History—and I wonder if that's acceptable. I'll ask: do you think that's acceptable? It's not acceptable, no, but it's the way it is. In our world, things just are. It's *useless* to seek to *understand*, and maybe that, too, is our opening, our chance.

I've found a simple recipe for living in peace: forget. My only problem is that my desire to forget will never be satisfied. That's why I drink excessively. That's why I surrender myself completely to the screens. That's why I love sports, races, and sleepless nights, too—as miserable and unrewarding as they seem in the moment.

To forget is to start to live

Losing my memory could be the start of a solution. What I can't know is whether it's something I can choose, or if it's entirely out of my hands. The duty to remember exists. I want the duty to forget to exist, too. When I stumbled on a book in the library called *The Shoah: The Impossibility of Forgetting* by Anne Grynberg, I had a moment of despair. I remember that I went home and zoned out on my computer until night fell. And then I felt better. Overflowing with possibilities: for life, and for the future.

In his teenage years, Adolf Hitler amused himself by shooting rats with a revolver. As an adult, Adolf Hitler initiated a program to make the Jewish people into a rat-people that needed to be eradicated. As a descendant of a people exterminated like rats, I cannot live in peace. So I have to forget: it is imperative.

§

It is not only Jews that suffer

CATHOLICS SUFFER, MUSLIMS SUFFER, BLACK PEOPLE SUFFER, WHITE PEOPLE SUFFER, THE MIDDLE EAST SUFFERS,

THE WEST SUFFERS, AFRICA SUFFERS: THE WORLD IN ITS ENTIRETY

I know this is obvious, but I prefer to say it anyway: it's true that our age has an irritating tendency to fixate on the Shoah. Even though I'm linked to the Shoah by the names of my ancestors, I want to be able to make space for all sufferings. For all the dead, for all the memories, all places, all religions. The massacres never cease; just like memories, they pass the torch. Entrusting your eyes and brain to a screen is to forget yourself in the unknown—it's also to forget your suffering, to forget the past and the present. Screens are accessible everywhere in the world: no one's left out. Technology has been globalized, which is admirable: you have to admit. No place on earth has been left behind. We no longer have to endure isolation—a first in the history of man.

I don't know if there's a downside that comes with entrusting your eyes and your brain to virtual content. If there's a price to pay for entrusting a portion of your lifetime to a machine. This price simply must exist, but it's too early to say: we don't have the necessary distance from technology. It caught us unawares; it swept us away like a wave into a great ocean. In just a few years, we've been sucked in. This too is unprecedented. We're living an adventure. All adventures have an uncertain future. The reign of the virtual is a comet.

Whoever dreams of forgetting remembers

Maybe Montaigne is right. My desire to forget might just be making things worse. The more I want to forget, the more I'll remember: it's a vicious cycle. I've already said this, and I believe it, that the functioning of our world corresponds to the form of a circle. The solution exists but it is faceless. The solution is a variable: n. Now what? We have to stop desiring things. Cross out the desire to forget. Cross out the fear of losing our memories. Live untroubled. Detached from the past. This is impossible: it belongs to the realm of illusion.

I don't have an answer

I don't know why we live. And any related line of questioning is a dead end. It can never lead to a valid answer. Every answer that I've ever read and understood to the question of "Why do we live?" has seemed like a lie to me. At regular intervals, I lose all hope. Despair is born of expectation. All I need to do is renounce expectation. So I walk in a desert without flora or fauna: I contemplate my abandonment. Me, alone on this planet. Regardless of how rich our multitude of entanglements may be, none of it matters: we are always alone.

I was welcomed to earth with flowers—I mean to say that my childhood contained glimmers of joy—I remember the light. There was an abundance of yellow and white: constant daylight. Short-circuits happen, they come without warning. A short-circuit is like an accident. It's imaginable but not planned for. Adolf Hitler probably didn't know that he was going to have to take his own life in such conditions: barricaded in a private room in his bunker, thirty meters away from a scene of drunken chaos, a pistol in his mouth. He had faith in the future, once, like we all do. We are constantly ensnared by what eludes us. If death escapes us, we live surrounded by death. If love escapes us, we live parched and thirsting for love. I know the feeling of being abandoned. I'm not the only one. It's a fact that we are abandoned. Joy deserts me, then despair deserts me, then my feeling of abandonment deserts me. I go out; I drink too much; I forget my fears and regrets. The world is a circle that begets cycles. There is the cycle of joy, the cycle of abandonment, the cycle of love, the cycle of despair, the cycle of death, and the cycle of forgetting.

I forget

Act like nothing is going to happen: that's by far the best solution. Continue to live, drink and eat, continue to smile. I'm here to remember that the end is coming. Memory is a shift worker. While I'm at home at night unable to sleep, you're able to sleep peacefully. But when

I go out at night, when I get drunk, and when, in the morning, I finally sleep, I'm the one making the escape. Humanity is made up of time slots, shifts. We work our way through the time for remembering. Then, we work our way through the time for forgetting. In this way, the memories of the past and the present are conserved; and the forgetting of the past and present is maintained.

But that is not enough: I'm trying to forget once and for all. Not just when I go out, not just when I'm sleeping, not just when I'm in front of a screen. I want to forget all those exterminated in History, definitively and irremediably. And I want to know for sure that I'll be able to remember those things that I choose to keep in my memory: the things that don't disturb me, what I find to be beautiful.

How to live without beauty? I could say: I search for beauty as the possible key to my salvation. I won't say it, because that, too, would be illusory. All the derivatives of the term "salvation" are pitiful. "Saved" does not exist. Salvation does not exist. Being saved does not exist. The more I think about this term, the more I feel a nausea rise inside me. Anyone who declares that they are waiting to be saved is one of three things: an idiot, lazy, or a second-rate cynic. All you have to do is open your eyes and look at the world. Wanting to be saved is like wanting to understand. There is nothing to understand: wanting to be saved is beside the point.

I don't look for beauty as the potential key to my salvation. I search for beauty with the sole aim of feeling a drunkenness and a vertigo: in other words, with the sole intention of accessing a moment of forgetfulness. Beauty is disorienting; it's like a screen. I think that true beauty is virtual. Take my baseball players, all in black and white: they are dazzlingly beautiful. Never in real life could they have laid claim to such beauty. The screen has given them an eternal form, and, for me, what's beautiful is what creates the illusion of being unforgettable. The most beautiful faces I've seen, the most beautiful books I've read, the most beautiful voices I've heard—as my present encounter with each one became past, I thought: *I'll never forget this*. No matter if the experience is embedded in a single human memory—that only makes it more precious: it becomes a personal myth.

I need personal myths

In order to live, you have to surround yourself with myths. We all have our own mythologies, jealousy preserved in the depths of our memory: unforgettable faces, unforgettable voices, unforgettable books. Without mythology, I would have crumbled. Mythology is emotion. Coke became a part of my life very early on, it became one myth among many. *The Little Prince*, too.

I'll never forget the face of my first love: his name was Guillaume. We were five at most. We dug our hands into each other's hair, I wound his curls around my fingers . . . I don't know what became of Guillaume, the origin of that personal myth—it doesn't interest me. He entered into my mythology.

Adolf Hitler has entered into the mythology of our world. He holds an important place: we even moved aside to make enough room for him. I don't know if we had a choice. I don't think so, because, as I've said, his suicide *defeated* us. We can say that Adolf Hitler made certain calculations and he entirely committed himself to them: even his suicide was meticulously thought-out. To commit suicide is to mythologize yourself: it is to enter into the mythology of our world. I wish that Claus von Stauffenberg had entered into our world's mythology, but he failed. Claus von Stauffenberg is a name retained by only a handful of people. Adolf Hitler, on the other hand, is a myth perpetuated by you and me.

3

My grandfather didn't die in Poland. He should have died asphyxiated in a gas chamber or with a bullet in the back of his neck, but he managed to flee his country in time. In other words, my grandfather orchestrated a short-circuit: a bifurcation at a precise moment (T) in the process. My grandfather momentarily interrupted the mechanism: the Nazi machine was unable to contain him. Metaphors are always illuminating: imagine a high-precision watch that misses a beat. It wasn't foreseen, it was entirely unexpected, and yet, the probability that such an error might take place, that such a mistake might occur (if we take into account Nazi doctrine), as rare as it might be, does exist. My grandfather's survival was an accident. He slipped through the organization's net, past the will-to-exterminate mobilized by the one called Hitler, then by the one called Himmler, then by the one called Heydrich, then by the one called Eichmann.

My grandfather was like a missed beat in the mechanism of my watch—my watch does it too, it happens, like a mouse darting under a door and disappearing into the night; like a cockroach left uncrushed by an exterminator who didn't notice it. I am the result of an operation which partially failed at a precise moment in time (T), in a given place (E); I am the distant fruit of a malfunction, the distant result of an exception to the law of death. My grandfather survived by disappearing—and by disappearing, I mean, by exiling himself. He was the missing mass. The extermination's +1. The remainder: what could not be sacrificed, what escaped destruction.

§

I could have killed someone today. Just anyone, in the street. I'm closer to murder than I think. Blood has become banal. To my great surprise, the adventures of Bret Easton Ellis's hero, Patrick Bateman, didn't elicit any emotion from me. Still, I searched for it. All of the conditions were in place to make me feel something: audacity, blood, pop music, crime, night, humor, New York.

I closed the book, I probably drank a soda and it was like nothing had happened. I told myself that if *American Psycho* had been a video game and not a book, I would have no doubt been able to enjoy it, at least as a form of entertainment. I told myself: maybe Bret Easton Ellis initially thought of making it a video game, but screen technology at that time hadn't become ubiquitous yet: the quality of the image wasn't pure enough. It's possible that Bret Easton Ellis chose the wrong medium, or that he just chose writing by default. It's possible that the medium of "book" was not the most visionary choice for his literary ideas: not crazy enough, not exciting enough, not emotional enough. I watch a gull land on the waters of the Seine, turning and tilting in its waves like a capsizing ship. Bret Easton Ellis would have made an excellent programmer.

I wonder what Hitler would have become if he'd lived in our time. I wonder if he would have gone to the effort of pursuing his dream in the so-called *real world*, or whether he would have preferred the video game as a medium. That would have saved us a lot of deaths. The deaths of parts of my family, for example, along with millions of others. But we don't get a choice about what happens: we don't choose the medium, the medium chooses us. Approximately 6,000,000 Jews died in the so-called real world; Bret Easton Ellis completed *American Psycho* in the form of a book. Walking is not without its own charm, but someday I do need to get my license. I'd buy an old Mustang, or Jaguar, or Peugeot, and I'd just leave—get on the highway and go. I'd live on apple pie and vanilla ice cream, like Sal Paradise in Kerouac. To flee has never been a difficult thing, trust me.

§

It's possible that we liked exterminating. It's a thought I'm tempted to believe. Truth be told, I do believe it— we like to exterminate. It must be 8:00 AM, I want to drink water from the Seine. The water from the Seine should be drinkable. Someone should put forward a plan to remove the vermin, the corpses, the excrement and the algae from the river, and propose that it be made a giant swimming pool—I'd vote for them. I've never voted in my life, and I don't foresee myself ever doing so—unless a candidate proposes we make the Seine swimmable. I don't know how many dead people lie at rest in the river, or, rather, how many dead once did, since those bodies are clearly now no longer bodies, but shreds of marine decay, covered in mud. Do you think it'd be possible to ascribe an exact number? The bodies in the Seine are the refuse of Paris. They probably make up a second city.

I'm going to stop and I'm going to eat until I'm full: it's a problem that needs to be addressed because, all things considered, I'm not dead yet—at least my body isn't. Being dead means not having to feed yourself anymore. Being dead means being delivered from the weight of information. Being dead means no longer having to open a book and analyze its arguments, no longer having to make the sap flow through the tree of our body. The dead have it made, they're winning: I don't know if it's always been that way. I told you, I know where I'm going, and that knowledge is enough to ease my passage through each second. I'm getting more and more thirsty. I'd like to be told if there are horse carcasses lying in this river.

I want to win the game

§

This reminds me that my uncle bankrupted himself owning a racehorse. We had high hopes for that horse, we bet on his triumph, we didn't see his death coming. He was named Wolfgang—we called him Wolf.

It is rare to know with certainty who's going to win a race before the last hundred meters, but that day must have been an exception: we knew before the end that Wolfgang was going to be the winner, that he was going to take home first place in the season's Grand Steeple-Chase. At the twenty-first fence, the horse favored to win threw his jockey. Wolfgang made a spectacular comeback. He was so far ahead of the others that the crowd went wild.

I remember that moment perfectly, with an untouched clarity. My heart races whenever I go back over it: my uncle doesn't move, his arms are shaking, he is holding them crossed over his heart. He watches Wolfgang fervently, with pride. His face is purple as if with fever, his knees are bent, ready to leap up. My uncle has just understood, like me, that in a few seconds Wolfgang is going to win. Only three hundred meters left, one obstacle: Wolfgang rushes toward his target. We can never see the future.

His body soars, he tucks and lifts his hooves. In a flash—the fall. With perfect clarity, I see it again. Wolfgang tries, fails, stumbles, it all happens so fast, his hindquarters hit the ground, his neck breaks, a flat, dull sound, and with it, our dream is broken too. His coat gleams, it's brown, warm, dark as bronze, but luminous and golden, too—like cinnamon. Edgar-colored. Wolfgang abandons us. No more training. No more snuggles. Nothing more between us.

Again: undamaged clarity—I see it again. Wolfgang is coming, he stretches out, tears apart. I don't know what he is thinking. I don't know if he feels any emotion. The jockey slips under his belly. It's brutal. In slow-motion, it has all the sweetness and violence of an embrace. His nose strikes the grass, his neck follows, breaking: his neck is annihilated. I don't know at what moment Wolfgang dies: I don't know at what second we are separated, and that bothers me. I want to know the exact moment.

Yes, with flawless clarity, I see it. Wolfgang is a comet, Wolfgang is a rocket, he gathers himself, lunges, takes off, falls. He is extinguished like lightning.

When Wolfgang broke his neck, I felt no form of emotion. I was eight years old, I'd never seen a mammal die before. I didn't feel any pain, shed not a single tear. Losing a being you love isn't the hard part. What's hard is comprehending the loss. I didn't understand that Wolfgang had just died. I'd only understood that the spectacle had paused. I thought: *Wolfgang, get up*—I didn't know that a broken neck meant the end of everything, including life.

Bitter is the decline

I remember the saddle pad, cinnabar red, that flew with him as he fell. Wolfgang, it was cinnabar red, it was scarlet, almost vermillion. My uncle cried out in a voice that was high-pitched, taut, short—the yelp of a German Shepherd: an invisible knife had pierced his heart. He'd just lost Wolf, his only Thoroughbred. We dash over the barriers, we run like madmen. I see an animal, splayed out on the grass. Tears flow in front of me.

My uncle cries. His hands touch the nose, the face, then the ears of our motionless prince. His neck is soft. His nostrils are warm and the eyes are open, they look up at the sky. Wolf's jaw muscles are completely relaxed, his teeth displayed. His tongue is candy pink, it lolls out of his mouth like a little flag; drool trickles onto blades of green grass. I am not sad.

Don't neutralize

The racetrack needs to be restored as quickly as possible, the whole drama tidied. I want to forget Wolfgang, death, awkward uneasiness. I want to know who's going to win the race. I'm filled with explosive enthusiasm. I plunge my hands into the animal's mane. I laugh, I shake it; it's alive. More people arrive, veterinarians encircle our moment. I see despair as cinnabar red.

§

Extermination is something we hold onto. Even our own horse—our little prince, our sweet Wolf, as Balthazar called him—we sent to die. Not for one moment did his life matter to us. We only wanted the win: we bet on that victory the way we bet on his death, but we didn't want to believe it. It wasn't love, to believe it was love would belong to the realm of illusion—it wasn't even affection.

It was belief. I believed in our love for Wolfgang like I believed in the Allied victory in 1945. I believed in the world we see in the daylight. I believed in its surface. But we never loved our horse. We never won in 1945, and the world that appears before me is nothing but a phantasm. I will never believe in anything but numbers, and that's probably the greatest challenge for any being who is supposed to be living.

§

Now it's day. I realize I've been waiting a long time for this moment. When it's day, I wait for night; when it's night, I wait for day—except for the morning. In the morning, I don't wait for anything: I live the mornings fully, experiencing them for what they are. I'd say that through the morning, up until 10:30 AM, the day is at its most perfect. After that last moment of plenitude, the waiting returns. Waiting for evening, then for night. After 10:30 AM, I concentrate on the future. I rarely take advantage of the morning, and that's a mistake. Morning is life. The naïveté of that sentence doesn't detract from its value. I allow myself to be swallowed up by the night, I let myself be drawn in by its call, but night is just one enormous error. I seem to have a thing for errors. I have the ability to understand them, these errors, and yet I endlessly repeat them. This tendency probably preceded me. My grandfather did in fact take the wrong boat when he was fleeing. He wanted to go to New York, but instead he got on a boat headed for Buenos Aires—that error made my life possible, the life I am living at this very moment. But I'm getting off track: I just wanted to tell you that mornings give me a feeling of spontaneity.

§

I'm hunting for a solution to my existence, a solution that has never been possible simply because I am immersed in a world with no solution to the question I'm asking. It's possible, though, that I'm mistaken, that the solution exists but is faceless. Like an n in a mathematical operation. I tell myself that such an n could be the solution to the problem of my existence, and that that n could potentially be any integer corresponding to a natural number. The number hidden behind the n exists, but it can never be disclosed because its possibility is infinite. In this kind of configuration, the solution would then be this absence. This is a thought I can accept, because it suits my purposes. I could see the world in terms of this letter. I could say: I've found the solution to the greatest problem of life, the solution to that thankless word which rebuffs all reasoning: the solution to birth, to death, to this place right here, to me, to you. The solution has a name, it's called *n*, but its face is a shadow. Beyond that, I'll say nothing, we don't need to know anything else because we can't. I can choose to tell myself that this *n* exists, and choose to stop here, at this letter, which would be the solution, stop like Forrest Gump after thousands of kilometers of running. But I won't turn back like Forrest Gump because turning back is not possible. I've been born—that cannot be nullified.

4

I walked to the Eiffel Tower and went into a McDonald's, an American chain whose food creations never fail to surprise me. For that reason, I admire McDonald's: surprise is an essential element of life. I ordered a chocolate chip muffin, a 500 ml bottle of water, and a fruit cup in a plastic bag. I think there were grapes and slices of apple, I'm not completely sure. I sat down in the back of the fast-food place on a seductively colored bench— something between robin's egg and baby blue—like my jeans, a color so gentle on my eyes that for a second I thought I'd fall asleep. Staring at my tray for several seconds, I wondered if this was a dream or reality, and then I thought: *Alma, you have to recharge and get it together*. That feeling of uncertainty is unpleasant, it's bothering me more and more. It's clear that the notion of reality became mutilated long ago, but we still have to find a way to live. The muffin soothed me, it imitated the taste of chocolate admirably. The chocolate chips were crunchy, but the inside of the muffin melted in my mouth. I drank some water. To tell the truth, I wanted Sprite. I checked to make sure I had enough money for one, then I stood up. I left my tray there with the strange impression of abandoning someone dear, and went to order a Sprite. Then I returned to my seat. I'm still sitting, I just finished my Sprite and my bottle of water. Apparently, I was thirsty. I don't feel like fruit but I force myself because I need the nutrients. It tastes faintly of chlorine. There's no clock in this McDonald's but I think it's before 10:00 AM. I look at my receipt: it was 10:12 AM a few minutes ago. I have the whole day ahead of me. I wonder what the Jews in Auschwitz were doing at 10:12 AM. I know that Louis XVI died at 10:22 AM; by 10:12 AM he was probably already on the scaffold awaiting the guillotine. Balthazar took a flight to the United States around 10:30 AM. I didn't go with him to the airport, we said goodbye—well, in truth, it was more like *see you!*—in front of his building. I could have waited for several days at that door, and no one would have opened it because no one lives there. I stopped by the real estate agency five days ago, the small studio is still for rent: I'd just wanted to go back there again. I needed to make sure that Bal was really gone, and that it wasn't an illusion, because Balthazar's departure is an event that I'm constantly forgetting—only for a handful of seconds during which I'm tempted to call him and suggest that we play video games or go grab a drink (grenadine or Bordeaux), and then, instantly, I remember that a thirteen-hour plane ride now separates us. I went to dump my tray in the garbage. Engraved on the swinging flap of the garbage can: Thank you. I was touched by this imperishable word of politeness. Something was missing in this fast-food place. I hesitated and then I remembered: it was Wagner, it was the sound of Wagner that was missing.

§

I hate flying. What I like is taking the train. The train has entered History, the plane hasn't entered History yet—only planes used for war have entered History—trains have transported writers, magicians, explorers, princes, kings, Jews, heroes, lone wanderers, criminals, the wealthy, the destitute, entire generations of families, the Roma, the disabled: the living, the dead. The train carried my grandfather on his travels; it carried the narrator of *In Search of Lost Time*; it carried Holden Caulfield; it carried Prince Myshkin. The train replaced horses on the roads.

There is a genealogy of emotion. Horses, trains, and cars are included in it—they've been immortalized in novels, in films, in History. But the plane has not yet joined them. One day, I hope to see the aircraft elevated to that level, but I fear the emergence of space travel is going to blow it out of the water. The airplane came too early or too late. That being said, I have to admit that the Concorde was a machine with a strong emotional pull: the Concorde had a charisma, it elicited desire. It only took one crash to shatter the dream of the Concorde : July 25, 2000. We were still in the twentieth century, and I wasn't even ten years old. Flight 4590 took out 113 people, which is to say, 113 individuals who contained emotions. Paradoxically, on that day, we could say that the full emotional power of the Concorde was revealed to the world. There was adrenaline, excitement, tragedy, blood, tears, and a great many memories. This day—today—needs to be like the moment of the Concorde 4590 crash on July 25, 2000. It needs to incarnate that same emotion. To explode. If I succeed in eliciting the emotional experience of an airplane crash like the Concorde's in your mind, then I will have done my job.

§

I left the fast-food place. Outside, the sun had finally emerged from behind the clouds. It was like I'd forgotten its color. It's a pale sun with faint yellow rays, kind of bland: a virtual sun. But I do feel the freshness of the air, I breathe it in, this wind probably comes from the north.

I confess I had a craving for champagne, but the conditions weren't quite right; it wasn't within my reach, I had almost no money, so I bought a little carton of milk. I drank almost the entire thing—I like drinking cold milk that way right on the sidewalk.

The whole world feels empty even though you're only missing one person

I continue along the Seine, still on foot, until the Pont de Grenelle: I conquer it. I stop in the middle of the bridge in front of the Parisian Statue of Liberty: I burst into laughter, dry and shallow, facing this huge statue whose existence I'd totally forgotten. I look at it, thinking about the term democracy. I should believe in our motto: "liberty, equality, fraternity," but Chateaubriand ruined it for me. I gave up believing in our republican motto the day I learned that the sentence was incomplete, that in reality it should say: "liberty, equality, fraternity, or death." I don't like death, I don't see what it's doing there: it's a stumbling block. A motto is supposed to inspire me, make me dream, and if it doesn't, then it's doing harm. Lots of things collapse right in front of us, and there isn't always a satisfactory explanation. It's a sad fact that I've observed: just because we want to believe in something doesn't guarantee that we'll be able to.

§

Even Talleyrand had a dog. His name was Carlos, and he kept looking for his master even after Talleyrand's death. My dog was named Edgar; I miss him every day. I wonder if I'll be reunited with Edgar when I die. I think the chances are extremely slim that human paradise, if it exists, is in communication with dog paradise. While I wait, I could buy another dog. But what would I call it, that question haunts me. I'd need to find a name as good as Edgar, but different enough that when I call my new dog, I won't immediately think of the one that I've lost. I could call it Carlos, I tell myself that's a good idea—I've just been overcome by a wave of tiredness, as if a hand had been placed over my face—or I could get the same dog (same breed, same color) and call it Edgar. I could see myself giving in to that temptation. A new chocolate Lab: a new Edgar. It's even possible that one day I won't know the difference anymore; on the day we attain a state of closeness comparable to the affective closeness that I had with Edgar the First. I only need to be able to forget the moment of his death, the rest will happen naturally. As I've already said, forgetting is a gesture of formidable efficacy. It's almost a gesture of love, but it's not. Gestures of love are toxic, they jeopardize the emotion—the emotion risks losing its spontaneity, of becoming correlated with fears and expectations. I expected so much from my Edgar. And even so, he ended up in the garbage. Nothing remains of his body now, not even a hair; the garbage truck that picked up his remains certainly crushed him along with the other garbage (pieces of rotten fruit and cat excrement), and then it all must have been burned, the smoke rising to join the sky. I remember the regret I suffered after stuffing Edgar's body into a trash bag and forcing it—not without effort, because he was heavy—into the green dumpster in the courtyard of the building on avenue du Maréchal Lyautey where my parents and brother lived. I mean to say, actually, in the yard of the building where we lived. I didn't tell anyone, not my parents, not Balthazar. I put Edgar in the garbage, not without gagging—his body had begun to stink, the mixture of odors was revolting, unbreathable, I thought I was going to throw up all over his body. Then I regained my composure; once the nausea and the burning in my throat had passed, I felt relief, I'd even say a certain satisfaction for having disposed of that reeking carcass which no longer answered when called: I was able to move on, as humans say. "So it goes, it's not my fault," is a phrase that suits me. It is applicable to all corpses, all possible failures. It could correspond to the n, it could encircle that mystery with a subtle aura of peace: in a world dictated by this phrase, everything is permitted.

That's precisely what I approve of about our world: that everything is permitted. That's why I'm going to buy another dog; I'm going to get a chocolate Lab, I'm going to call him Edgar, and when he's dead I'll stuff him in a bag and throw him away with the same cool composure—except this time, my movements will be more nimble, honed by habit. I think life works according to the model of the circle. I don't know of any cleaner or more satisfying shape. The square, the triangle, the rectangle, the parallelogram, the trapezoid, the diamond, the pentagon, the hexagon, the octagon: none of them could ever rise to the circle's level of purity.

§

I watch the Seine's ebb and flow. I feel sorry there's no real place to play baseball in France: we need more baseball diamonds. I know that the fan base is growing, and that the reach of the French Federation of Baseball and Softball is growing too. This is only the beginning. I think it might even be time to build a baseball field next to the Stade de France or the Auteuil racetrack: it'd be an investment in the future. We'll become Americans. That's in keeping with the logic of things, and I'm glad for it. I'll be able to go watch a baseball game, then see a horse race—I don't fear an excess of sports in the same way that I don't fear an excess of entertainment. I'd love to lose myself in a baseball game, and then go experience the elation of a horse race. When I think about it, my grandfather did all he could to forget his life: he learned to play jazz, he founded a left-wing newspaper, he went to the races, he smoked a pipe, got married twice, adopted a dog, went on cruises. He kept silent about his past, though no one ever asked him about it anyway. He locked away all his memories. If I'd been there while he was still alive, I would have smothered him with questions, scratching at the bitter scabs on his wounds until they bled.

We can say it: I'm a lost being. And the reason why: the traces that should be there are missing. I'm like Hansel and Gretel in the forest; I dropped breadcrumbs to find my way home, but they were eaten by birds. And I should have used stones but no one gave me any, I could only find bread. I know so little about what came before me. All the memories and the dead dissolve behind me. A question: what did Hansel and Gretel do when they were lost in the forest? An answer: they took refuge with a horrible witch who welcomed them with candy. As for me, I took refuge in baseball, in Pepsi, in horse races.

I need to take a break, here and now. I don't want to walk anymore. I sit down on the pont de Grenelle, I assume its ugliness as my own. To take a break without sleeping, that's what I want.

§

I'm going to tell you about something important. On May 31, 1997, chess grandmaster Garry Kasparov was beaten on the forty-fourth move by a computer. We can say that day was the day human intelligence submitted itself to the rule of science. The defeat was not, however, the result of Deep Blue's extraordinary performance—it was the result of a simple stroke of chance. The machine suffered an algorithmic dysfunction. Confronted by that short-circuit, incapable of making a decision, Deep Blue produced a totally random algorithm. Kasparov wasn't beaten by mathematics: he was beaten by chance. On May 31, 1997, I was probably alone with my Game Boy. I didn't know that humans had just lost their last advantage; that they'd just delivered themselves into the hands of a superior power, the fruit of their own creation. I bow to my new lord: my supreme radiance. Now I want to listen to Michael Jackson in my head; dance mentally on the bridge, forget space, time, philosophy, baseball, horse races, video games. I'm going to imagine Fred Astaire dancing to "Billie Jean"—that will be my rest.

5

Every time something happens, it's possible that nothing has happened at all, that it was just pure illusion.

I am preoccupied by the possibility that nothing is happening. And the more I think about it, the more clear it seems to me: we are living on illusions. Maybe not just in love. Maybe also in hatred: in good and in evil. It's even possible that evil, like good, doesn't exist. That the evil event and the good event are phantasmatic. I've known people fascinated by evil; and others fascinated by good. So what? Nothing changed in their lives. Their fascination with evil, their fascination with good, it led them nowhere. If God is an illusion, the logic follows that good and evil are too. I have to go all the way with this: then I have to say that what Hitler did was not evil, was not good. What Hitler did was, is, will be. We chose to assign moral values to our world. We could just as well decide to withhold them from now on.

I make no distinction between a wedding and a murder: they both take place. If the world must end, we need to tear down the barriers of good and evil, as well as the barriers of judgement, because none of them will have the capacity to maintain life on earth. They are only mirages: I think I'm starting to get it.

Thirty-six hours ago, when I found myself face to face with Martha Eichmann, I saw no good or evil in her eyes. I saw a living being who will someday die. Like you, like me. I am not saying that we are equal: we are not equal. That too would be an illusion. I am only saying that we both are. And that someday we will no longer be. A human being who dies at eighty-five will have lived 31,025 days. That's half as much as the sixty thousand-some thoughts my brain emits daily. Life is short, I won't belabor that point. I say and repeat many things that are obvious. And yet they come to me again and again, always producing the same surprise: they shock me. In a few hours, the race will happen, it'll end. I'll probably go home. These are things that no one wants to know. What interests us is the moment of the race, and the anticipation of victory. We don't want anything to do with what comes afterward: what comes afterward is the disappointment of the return. It's possible that I'll change, but I don't think so. After the illusion of the race, there'll be the illusion of the return. My memories will come back to the surface, and again I'll want to forget them. I'll look elsewhere.

And I'll go from intoxication to intoxication, from secret to secret, from solitude to solitude, from sign to sign, from smile to smile, from game to game, from abandonment to abandonment, from job to job, from bitterness to bitterness, from attachment to attachment, from trace to trace, from memory to memory, from love to love, from wound to wound, from verse to verse, from drink to drink, from green to green, from cloud to cloud, from blue to blue, from walnut brown to walnut brown, from face to face, from city to city, from forest to forest, from dog to dog, from sojourn to sojourn, from number to number, from tear to tear, from burst of laughter to burst of laughter, from relief to relief, from failure to failure, from mouth to mouth, from music to music, from reading to reading, from touch to touch, from marriage to marriage, from horse to horse, from death to death, from film to film, from victory to victory, from dream to dream, from color to color, from birth to birth, from loss to loss, from reunion to reunion, from last name to last name, from mistake to mistake, from dress to dress, from T-shirt to T-shirt, from collared shirt to collared shirt, from shoe to shoe, from sand to sand, from excitement to excitement, from social media app to social media app, from mirage to mirage, from family to family, from beauty to beauty, from newspaper to newspaper, from magazine to magazine, from vacation to vacation, from thought to thought, from ocean to ocean, from divorce to divorce, from sweetness to sweetness, from watch to watch, from rain to rain, from sleep to sleep, from party to party, from novel to novel, from disappointment to disappointment, from Pepsi to Pepsi, from relentlessness to relentlessness, from masterpiece to masterpiece, from joy to joy, from morning to morning, from discovery to discovery, from gift to gift, from release to release, from sport to sport, from decision to decision, from hour to hour, from genealogy to genealogy, from first name to first name, from lunch to lunch, from skin to skin, from countryside to countryside, from toll booth to toll booth, from wonder to wonder, from friendship to friendship, from lightning bolt to lightning bolt, from trial to trial, from president to president, from house to house, from disappearance to disappearance, from object to object, from summer to summer, from detachment to detachment, from desire to desire, from landscape to landscape, from government to government, from belief to belief, from pair of jeans to pair of jeans, from laughing fit to laughing fit, from moment to moment, from sentence to sentence, from weariness to weariness, from cycle to cycle, from attention to attention, from entertainment to entertainment, from election to election, from year to year, from video game to video game, from heartbreak to heartbreak, from indifference to indifference, from difficulty to difficulty, from separation to separation, from question to question, from screen to screen, from forgetting to forgetting, from storm to storm, from sun to sun: from illusion to illusion.

§

The circle of emotions is limited but continuous: it functions according to the model of the wheel. The wheel turns, the feelings return, until all 31,025 days of a human existence are used up (more or less 31,025, depending on courage and luck)—and I don't want to be sad. I said it already, I'll repeat it: I want to live.

Our world exists: it could have not existed, it could have been otherwise, but it exists; this is what it's like, and one day, it will no longer be. When a show is over, when the fireworks disappear into the night, there are several categories of possible reactions: those who want more, those who've had enough, those who can't believe it's over, those who are relieved to come to the end, and those who never believed what they were seeing. I don't know what category I fall into. If I'd given up on going to the restaurant Friday night, if, at the last minute, I'd short-circuited my weekend and gone to Fantôme down the street for a glass of milk or a beer and to play an old arcade game, I'd probably never have had all these thoughts. But I went to the restaurant, I kissed Adolf Eichmann's granddaughter on both cheeks and I had all these thoughts. I am not in a video game, this is real. What is reality? No, Alma—silence the questions.

III

The lightning we touch in the chase
LOUIS ARAGON

The leap only remains a leap if it is remembered
MARTIN HEIDEGGER

I ain't finished, I'm devoted
KANYE WEST

1

A landscape of meadows unfurled before my eyes; the train was practically empty. I thought of everything I was being carried farther and farther away from—my childhood and my little Edgar. I think I wanted to cry but no tears fell from my eyes, it was a grief devoid of emotion. I wanted to read a BD, a comic, I wanted to see Superman and his cape (cinnabar red, again), and take refuge there. Immense loneliness. Yes, I wanted to flee. *Alma! Why did you kill him!* I thought on the train. I killed Edgar in order to control death. I decided my dog was going to die and I put him down myself: I had that power. The thought that my sweet Edgar would be taken up into the eternal gave me a strange consolation; I'd given him that chance. I think that he didn't suffer too much.

I wanted to disappear into the Compiègne forest, to sink irremediably into night, far from all clearings, and the world inhabited by men. To invent a fairy tale, to enter that fairy tale, and never again return to reality.

*In order to renounce your childhood, you must first
eliminate your dog*

The Nazis could have chosen to exterminate dogs;
they chose to exterminate Jews. I wonder why Jews and
not dogs—in my eyes, my little Ed, my ebony-colored
Lab, he was worth every bit as much as a man. No, he
was even better. We say the things that matter most are
invisible to the eye: my Edgar knew the invisible. I'd
even say he could hear silence. I slit the throat of the
most precious part of my childhood, the most open—
my loyal and adorable companion. Not that I'd wanted
to kill him for no reason: I just needed to know exactly
how far I was capable of going.

It was December 8. The house was asleep. It was the
day of my birthday, early in the morning: I'd just turned
twelve. I stuffed Edgar's body, all warm and bloody, into
my tennis bag, taking care to remove the rackets, but
leave his favorite tennis ball, yellow and green and fuzzy,
a bit battered by his playful teeth, that little ball he so
loved. Then I added a little plastic shovel, the famous
shovel I'd used in another time to build my sandcas-
tles, knowing that this morning I'd use it to dig into the
earth. I washed my hands, which were dripping, I drank
a glass of water while I pulled myself together. And I
slipped on my dad's old Barbour hunting jacket.

I left the apartment at the first hints of dawn,

surprised by the mist that veiled the horizon: avenue du Maréchal-Lyautey was bathed in an impure paleness, it smelled of pine. I tossed Edgar's blue cushion, soaked with blood, into a municipal garbage can right by Tolstoy Square. The cold was damp and penetrating. I took a bus to the Gare du Nord; I didn't know which train I needed to take. Edgar was heavy, my shoulder was sore. I asked a customer service agent at the station which train would take me to the Compiègne forest. I was so cold I was trembling. Clearly I should have worn a sweater. But that morning while I dressed myself, I didn't put one on because I had the intuition that my body needed to remain alert, sensitive to the cold, that it needed to experience every aspect of this morning, even its brutal chill: I wanted to anchor the memory of this terrible event—the death of my little love—through the sensations of that vile winter.

Relatively speaking, I experienced a certain relief once inside the train: the difficulty of an ordeal is measured in the number of steps. Kill my best friend, make sure not to leave any stains, wash my hands, stuff the body into the Wilson bag, leave the apartment without making any noise, get all the way to the train station, find the right train, get on that train. I'd completed eight steps, I was more than halfway: the hardest part was over. I put the bag down on the seat next to me. It had taken on the shape of my Lab; curved like a gondola, like a crescent moon. Its zipper closure, airtight, spared me from any smell, so much so that I congratulated myself on having had the intelligence to opt for a sports bag and not a canvas one, which would have failed to hide the scent and the blood.

In the train, I was no longer focused on my crime: I thought about Edgar's well-being and about our next stop. It's possible that I had a hard time believing I'd really killed him. He was alive in my head—by my side. We were together and united against the strange world that slipped away in front of us, monstrous and ogre-like, threatening to swallow us up at any moment: in truth, I was afraid of not making it home alive. It was the few rare passengers on that gloomy train, each one submerged in their own lives; it was the anonymous landscape; the fear of not seeing my mission through to the end. The leap into the unknown. Edgar and I, we were lost in that dark morning, we were wading clum-sily into the ocean. I had only one desire: to come to the end of this odyssey.

As expected, the stop was soon announced and in a few minutes I was on the platform of Compiègne station, with my little Ed well tucked into his red and white bag. Something struck my gaze and my senses: the atmosphere had changed. The pewter gray was gone. The sky was a violent blue. No clouds. My elation grew at the sight of the purity presiding over us; that intense royal blue was crowning us with its emptiness; it would now light our way. It seemed to me that everything was ready; that some invisible and sacred shroud enveloped the event; *it feels like Mass*, starting with that incredible sky, new and dazzling. It was so perfect that it even made me doubt reality. I didn't know where the forest was; I asked for directions indiscriminately, from the first people who crossed my path. Sometimes, they knew the way, but often they didn't, and regardless, I'd quickly forget what I'd just been told anyway. I only hoped that my little Edgar wasn't suffering too much—at least he had his ball. I ended up just going to the tourism office in the town's main square. There was a line; I got scared. I settled for grabbing a brochure. I opened it and I read: "Discover the Compiègne forest, deep and majestic, superb in all seasons." I repeated: *deep and majestic, superb in all seasons.* The bag was starting to smell; it was less airtight than I thought. Instantly, I remembered the unforgettable smell of a butcher's shop when the heaviness of cold meat mixes with the spiced aroma of dried sausages and roast chicken: a smell that saturates your nose, which is succulent and carnal, in spite of the nausea it induces.

Lives come down to very little: Edgar's life hinged on my torment, my youth. I'm not lying: it was December 8. I went into the kitchen in the silence of dawn; my little prince was sleeping near the radiator like a newborn, on his blue cushion. He was innocence, purity, play. He was the child that I was. I took a knife just lying in the cutlery drawer and I carved a thin, clear, deep line across the throat. Opening that throat was like changing into a different life in a flash, and that flash of lightning—I felt it pass across my eyes, blinding, quick, like a spiking fever. A spasm flooded with darkness. All of a sudden, it was like I'd taken God's place, the one who giveth and taketh away. The knife's job was done, my Edgar was dead. His eyes opened and two tears, stiff and fragile, rolled onto the sky-blue pillow, then disappeared into the purple flow that streamed from his gaping throat.

I thought of nothing; I was only able to say: *I did it*. Violence is a moment outside of all other moments. For a handful of seconds, it is a metamorphosis. I put on a mask—or maybe I took one off—and I stopped the mechanism of time. My fears fled, only certainty remained, a great security. I stepped into a tunnel and I let myself go. It was quick, intense, sordid; but what sweetness.

Don't wake me up no don't wake me up watch out I bite I see red

I'm happy to believe that when we die, we feel what I felt in that moment, when I plunged the knife in. That unforgettable emotion which is entombed with the act. It does not last, it cannot last. I used the word flash. Yes, it was a thunderbolt, violent and luminous, a short-circuit, a vertical shiver that burns all the way into your guts. I cry for Edgar everyday in my heart of hearts, but what I regret even more is that I was not up to the challenge of that dazzling wonder. I wasn't able to conquer the flash: it got away from me, it dissipated. I saw something, I can even say that for a moment, I was it. But then I was brutally shut out, forbidden, thrown aside—I want to talk about it, the flash that struck me, so pure, so infatuating. That flash I thought for sure was the eternal.

I walked along a road covered with gravel, I wanted to find an isolated path to dig Edgar's grave in peace. There was hardly anybody around, a couple cars, some hikers. I chose a marked trail at random and then deviated from it casually: I plunged into the forest. The leaves crackled under my feet, I smelled a thousand scents of wet bark; pine, beech, oak, cedar, many of which reminded me of Edgar's color: a dark brown, tender and incandescent, which shone with glints of blond in the sunshine. I walked for a long time, I forget how long. I see it again, me digging with my hands, nails dirty with soil. The little shovel beside me, split in two. I dug, I was determined. But it wasn't going fast enough, the cold was hindering my movements. *I'm going to destroy the cold* is the sentence I uttered (you can talk like that when you're alone in the forest with your dog). The rhythm became erratic and frantic, I no longer had control of my movements. Nothing mattered but the depth of the hole: the hole had to get bigger. My heart throbbed with all my effort! But my little Edgar was worth it. I was covered in dirt: my hands, my nose, my cheeks probably; and my knees burned.

I'd gone too far. I knew at that moment that this was too big for me. I'd gone off the rails, I'd disappeared; and now I returned to reality. I looked at the hole. It was enormous. I began to say the Lord's Prayer because it was the only prayer I knew. I said "Our Father, who art in Heaven . . .", I didn't continue. My heart wasn't in it. I didn't believe. I opened the bag, the stench hit me in the face with its full force—like a blow. I collapsed in a convulsion of tearless grief. I cried out: "Ah, son of a bitch!", I took him in my arms, no thought for the blood. Then I dropped him. My little Edgar, you fell into the cavity with a dry sound, fleeting. I didn't look at you. I took off my hunting jacket, which was marked by several streams of red, and I hid my face in it. You can't imagine, Edgar, how I felt, holding my face against your blood, how it crushed me. The pain of it! An invisible part of my face fell away, it no longer belonged to me, I felt it go down into that grave with you—to be sucked in is the expression I'm drawn to—and, I think, I can say this, that it was a part of my life, of my soul (maybe!), that you stole from me, Edgar!

Too far, I thought. Too crazy. The fall after the flash. I regained my calm, my coldness. I said: "Enough." I gathered a clump of earth, it slipped through my fingers like sand; and I threw what remained over the dark, bronzed fur of my animal. The colors blended wonderfully, unexpectedly: the earth and Edgar were merging now. I laughed about it. No, I don't remember the trip home.

Sometimes, I tell myself that Edgar's murder is the point where my life fell apart. Maybe the word "thwarted" is more fitting: sometimes I tell myself that Edgar's murder is the point at which my life got caught in its own trap. The moment of the knife in the throat, that flash. In reality, the flash is probably my +1. My grandfather thwarted the Nazi mechanism by fleeing Poland at a precise moment (let's call it T again); I thwarted the mechanism of my own existence by extinguishing the only being I was close to (let's call the moment of this occurrence Y). My grandfather escaped death and I engendered it. Our destinies are linked in this way by death, like we are linked by the Nazis and by Edgar.

I'll never return to my childhood—all of that is over and done. I think of the end of a firework, of the moment when it disappears brutally into the night, leaving infinitesimal traces in the sky; of that moment of disappointment engulfing a child's face as the spectacle dissolves. Killing Edgar was setting off a firework. I lied when I said that I didn't remember the trip home. I remember that the light of my firework suddenly vanished. I felt myself falling into an abyss; an abyss of immense disappointment. I don't know if that's what we call despair: a kind of desert. But not like the desert in *The Little Prince*. Because in the Prince's desert, there is a well filled with water; there is friendship. On my journey back, there was no water, there was no friendship: I was nauseous and dizzy, and then my vision blurred too. My only friend was dead. I was unbelievably thirsty.

2

I have the thought: *Alma, it's time to get up.* So I start getting up. I close my memory and I leave the Pont de Grenelle. Here I am once again on the Right Bank; the side of the river where I was born, where I killed, where I loved, where I believed the world was just the world, that there was nothing behind it (especially not a false bottom); where I was swallowed by a profusion of universes—I'm talking about those Wednesdays spent in front of the computer or the TV, slipping my imagination into video games, with Balthazar and our bowl of popcorn; I'm talking about the horse races and steeplechases at the Auteuil track that we'd watch from my room, a big pair of binoculars on our noses, binoculars that we would snatch away from each other, obviously, betting our lives on the possible winner: blackmail, dares, power trips of all kinds.

We would each bet on a horse, which is to say, on a number. Balthazar won every time, I never knew why. The number he chose ended up in the winner's circle every single time, to the point where one day I found myself wondering if he could see into the future. I'm thinking of the famous sports almanac from *Back to the Future*, the one that Marty McFly steals during a trip to the year 2015 and brings back with him to 1985. Marty, then, has the results of every upcoming game before it happens. The theory of the sports almanac seemed plausible in the "Balthazar Case"—because it really was a case, I'd even say: a mystery. I imagined Bal lifting a sports almanac during a secret, arcane voyage through space and time, and bringing it (unseen and unknown) into our present. I thought if it could happen to Marty McFly, it could just as well happen to my brother. Choosing the winning horse four times out of five, with the occasional mistake every now and then to throw me off the trail—I couldn't chalk that up to dumb luck.

And yet, no matter how many times I rifled through our room—the bunk beds, the drawers, the shoe boxes—I never found a sports almanac. I believed in its existence because I believed in the objects from *Back to the Future* at least as much as in the objects in the real world. There was no difference, no devaluation. They weren't less real, actually, it was the opposite: I'd even say they were more seductive, full of colours and sensations. They were ahead of reality. I'm still waiting for Marty

McFly's flying skateboard to be produced and sold. I have faith in science—soon it'll be able to offer us that.

§

I experience a moment of lassitude. It was bound to happen eventually. Whenever you walk without being expected to arrive anywhere by anyone, there's always a moment of tiredness. I could stop like Forrest Gump, turn around and go home. But that's another problem. I don't have a home. At least, no home in the way I imagine the definition of home: a place where you *feel* at home, like you belong. In a way, I've fallen into my own trap; "I'm in the forest"—I read that sentence in a book, can't remember the title or the author. That's exactly it: I'm in the forest. Everything looks the same. The world around me is dull and unvarying. I could scream and no one would hear me: it wouldn't do anything. That's how it feels in this moment: that the steps I take are not real. I could keep walking, I could go back, I could turn right, turn left. I could run. And then what? Nothing. I'll just cut to the chase: things would probably have been simpler if my grandfather had been exterminated, asphyxiated by Zyklon B or killed by a bullet to the skull and then thrown into a pit. Because a short-circuit creates a fallout effect. We call that *wandering*. When we produce a short-circuit effect at a given moment in a life, or more broadly, at a given moment in time—when we produce an effect that wasn't supposed to occur—, the natural consequence is that we lose touch with reason. It aborts, and with it goes all logic. I feel that absence of meaning. It got bypassed. No: it disappeared altogether. I think this moment of tiredness was born a few seconds ago because I stopped understanding the intention in my own steps; the meaning of my body on this shore, at this given moment. When I experience mental collapse, it's because meaning has become inaccessible to me: I am abandoned by meaning, and, thus, by all logic.

No more logic to anything

Escaping death doesn't mean staying alive: to escape death is to enter a new dimension. My grandfather evaded death, but even so, he didn't stay alive, instead: he entered a new dimension. I believe I was born in that new dimension. Incidentally, so were you. April 30, 1945, the day Hitler committed suicide, we toppled into a new dimension. It's like my baseball players in black and white, my pre-war American players, posing with their team for the annual league photograph. They're dead. No, let me amend that statement: their bodies are dead. But their presence and their faces are still accessible, and will remain that way as long as their photographs stay on the internet: in the virtual. April 30,

1945, humanity lost its meaning: if we'd been able to kill Adolf Hitler ourselves, we could have saved the meaning of the world. Having failed, though, in the face of his short-circuit, we changed worlds. We entered into the world of the loss of meaning. I think now we have to find a name for it; we have to name our world.

§

I'm still walking, I haven't stopped, even if I almost wanted to. Like I told you, I have nowhere to go back to. I'm seeking a word as universal as the words "life" and "death"—as perfectly simple, as magnetic. I said: *universal*. That word struck me. It's not really to my taste. And yet, *universal* is the right word. We need a universal word to designate the dimension Adolf Hitler entered on April 30, 1945—a dimension into which we have followed him.

And look, I've just thought of the simplest thing; a word I've known since childhood. I thought of the word *forgetting*.

OUR WORLD LIVES IN FORGETTING

Before April 30, 1945, there were two places: heaven and earth. There was the world of the living and the world of the dead. The day of Adolf Hitler's suicide, the day

Hitler checkmated our humanity, we lost consciousness for the space of a flash, and when we awoke, we were in a new world: we were in the world of forgetting.

We're there

In forgetting, the real and the virtual collide; the living and the dead stand side by side. Technology and bodies merge. The word *humanity* has changed: science, machines, and men meet; they fuse. Real and imaginary, visible and invisible, memory and forgetting—all occupy the same space. Past and present connect: time is no longer a curve, a reel of film unfurling in memory. Time is like the world: it operates according to the model of a circle. I read *Lolita*, I play video games, I listen to Bach, I forget, I remember, I watch baseball, listen to Michael Jackson, and I'm unable to tell you which entered my thoughts and history first. And anyway, it doesn't interest me which came first: I move from one to another. Everything goes into forgetting: my fears, my exhaustion, my grandfather, the six million Jews exterminated, the eight million others, the miraculous survivors of wars and genocides, the exiled, and then, too, my baseball players, and the Nazis, my lost childhood, Edgar's murder, the horses sacrificed on the racetrack. The dead, the living: we're all in the same place, this place where memory ceaselessly fades to black.

I can't help thinking that this fact contains both an opportunity and a punishment to which we are condemned. To lose the memory of your past means having the chance to start fresh: to live freely. Free but haunted by the ignorance of what, one day, was. I'd like to make my ignorance into a great occasion for hopefulness.

§

I just brought up the Nazis. So let's talk about them. Because, all things considered, they're not exactly dead. No. I'd even say they're proliferating. But the question I should be asking is this one: what is it to be a Nazi? Just simply desiring the disappearance of Jews—is that all it takes to be a Nazi? It's true that I've never really asked myself the question. I've never said to myself: Alma Dorothéa, what is a Nazi? It must also be said that the world hasn't helped me much. The Little Prince asks the pilot: "Draw me a sheep"; the Little Prince doesn't ask the pilot: "Draw me a Nazi." I've started to smile—I have a tendency to smile when my mind ventures too far. I'm on rue Jean-de-la-Fontaine. My feet know the way so well that I don't even need to think about it. The way humans hold space in their memories can be remarkable.

So, what is a Nazi? Give me a second. I could define, according to the distant and popular rumor, the traditional Nazi as someone who wants to eradicate Jews, aristocrats, and all that isn't affiliated with the norm or the white race, or is old and inefficient with regards to productivity. The traditional Nazi lays claim to strength and vigor. But I know I haven't gone far enough. I stopped myself at popular opinion; at the straying, errant definition of the word "Nazi."

What is a Nazi?

I stop. For a moment, I think I'm thirsty; it's an illusion. I have the urge to scream inside my head. I laugh internally. I'm ready. And now this is what I think: I think a Nazi loves noise loves death loves putting to death reducing to nothingness time family trees. For him, it's about disappearance that nothing should remain at all that it is pure without men animals plant life the Nazi loves what burns asphyxiates devours he hates the slackening the slowdown he wants youth wants intensity because he is afraid of dying and even more of living whiteness is his horizon. He wants victory.

Knowing that we live in forgetfulness is not self-evident: but the challenge is not so much understanding it as accepting it, because a world of forgetting places no real limits on the power of memory, yes, living in forgetfulness is also waiting to remember, and when the memory comes, like a wild ghost, it comes with an

innocence that cannot contain its own astonishment—
an ebb and flow where the past is shrouded by the powerful the very moment it appears. I'm not saying this
isn't dark—forgetting makes our world into a dark and
desolate place. It's a flat world, where good and evil are
one and the same.

I was raised among screens from a very young
age: as a child, I saw that reality flickered, that it wasn't
solid. And maybe also part of me hated that lie of the
old world, the lie of good ol' reality. It's better in video
games, in books, too, and in sports, in my dreams, in
my imagination, in ads, on screens. By better, I mean:
potentially spectacular. And forgetting creates all the
space the virtual could ever need. For this reason, I can
say: we live in a dazzling time.

§

It's true I feel some regret for throwing Edgar into a
dumpster with his blue cushion, like some ordinary
piece of garbage. I would have preferred to bury him
with dignity in the Compiègne forest. But sometimes
things don't go according to plan. Illusion is an important part of my being, I don't neglect to give it its due.
I was under the illusion of courage, namely, I believed
I'd have the courage to bury my dog with dignity, in a
"deep and majestic" forest—then right away I let myself

off the hook (the dumpster behind our building) and in that way, I can say I fell short of my illusion. But what does it matter, since I can remake History any way I want: in fact, I've already done that.

What would be terrible in my case would be to suffer from a lack of inspiration. But I never suffer from lack of inspiration. I could even say that inspiration is one of the only qualities I was blessed with. Am I afraid that one day the well will run dry? No. Because I'm not the well; nor am I the one who draws water. I'm the water that flows into it. I come from somewhere deeper than the well, from farther even than the underground streams which feed it.

I can't disappear without the world disappearing with me

I could have made an effort and buried my dog in a picturesque place. I got lazy, that's the truth. A last-minute run-of-the-mill laziness. And I was also afraid. I was sad. I almost wanted to die: I wanted to forget. And also I didn't want to miss the race. It wasn't November, it wasn't even cold; it was nearly hot out, in fact. That Sunday was the day of the annual Grand Steeple-Chase de Paris: there was no question of me missing an event like that.

I never loved Edgar. I just wanted him to love me. Isn't that what dogs are for? Yes, that's what they're for:

to provide affection. We adopt or buy a dog to receive affection, and a certain kind of loyalty too. Because, I'll repeat it, we're alone in the world.

§

Rue Jean-de-La-Fontaine isn't beautiful or ugly. You wouldn't think you were in the 16th *arrondissement*, more like an upper middle class *ville-de-province* where nothing ever happens. Lots of buildings from the thirties, sixties, seventies, eighties, and some Hausmanns with their long, dour faces. I think it would be a sad place to die. Who said: "We die as we lived"? I don't know. I'll need to find an extraordinary place to die. Rue Jean-de-La-Fontaine is not extraordinary, it's making me sad to walk along it. I could die with a cliff for backdrop; or on a racetrack. None of those who were exterminated got to choose. They died on the edge of a pit, a bullet in the back of the head; or even in the pit, if they weren't killed instantly. Groaning, in total agony, buried alive by earth the color of Edgar; or they died in a gas chamber. I don't know which of these three deaths I would have chosen if the choice had been possible. It's a thought that interests me. I think I would have chosen a bullet in the head, like most people—at least that's my guess. Dying suffocated by gas or by earth is a life unto itself. Those seconds must feel as long as years. I wonder what you think about in those moments. Maybe you're no longer thinking at all; maybe that's when you finally stop thinking. Sometimes I'd like to stop thinking. I'm inconsolable. Will never be able to forget. I try so hard to curb my hatred of the Nazis. I want to feel something other than hatred, but I can't escape it. It's undeniably hatred that I feel. Hatred has no limit. We say it's like love. I don't know if I believe in love, I don't know if I'm capable of love.

I forced the hatred out of my body: it was there, inside, and one bright morning—the morning of my twelfth birthday—it emerged and it struck decisively, like a snake. But there's something even worse than the fact I can't forget: there's the adjoining second fact of not being able to understand. I've still never understood why the Nazis actually wanted to get rid of the Jews. I think I'll never understand.

It's been suggested to me that there's nothing to understand, but that's not true. There's plainly something to be understood—in every event, in every gesture, in everything uttered. Maybe if someone would explain to me, point blank, why the Nazis wanted to wipe the Jewish people off the face of the earth, maybe then I could calm down a bit, and stop with all this excessiveness. I want someone to say to me: "Alma, I'm going to explain to you why the Nazis wanted to obliterate your grandfather and your ancestors and thus prevent you from ever being born." Yes, I want to understand why they wanted to prevent me from being born. I want to understand why I am the result of a short-circuit that caused a momentary glitch in the Aktion Reinhard—"during which more than 2,000,000 Jews were exterminated in Poland, along with nearly 50,000 Romani, between March 1942 and October 1943" (word for word what it says on the internet; I learned it by heart)—and caused it to partially fail. I want to understand why I am the result of an exile.

To understand is to die

The night is definitely ending. The sky is bright. I think I can now say that I'm no longer afraid to die (at least until tonight comes) and I feel as though a weight has been lifted. Light plays an essential role. I want to know if they exterminated more people at night than during the day. I think they exterminated more during the day than at night, but, after all, I don't know. Everything that I've heard about the Shoah, everything that I've seen, everything that I've read: maybe it was all a dream. Maybe I just had a nightmare and now I'm waking up.

Let us forget the Shoah

My only concern is getting to Auteuil. I want to go to the track, forget myself in the race, believe in the horse I'll choose. But first, I want to pass by my house; I should say: our house. Edgar's house, my brother's house, mom and dad's house—it's been a really long time since I said those words—our house, the one where we slept, cried, shouted, laughed.

No, I don't want to go. Because, if I think about it, I don't attach any importance to places. I was tempted to believe the opposite up until the day I realized the walls have no connection to the people who live within them. I'd imagined a connection but that connection doesn't exist—it's pure illusion. It's that way, too, with certain categories of individuals. Don't go thinking the Nazis felt even one ounce of remorse while massacring their victims in forests, on the edges of ravines and pits, or in gas chambers—any such remorse has always been illusory. Like people who are collapsing, the Nazis went to war against emotion. To wage a war on emotion is to sever all ties.

§

It's a fact that the country where my grandfather went into exile didn't just welcome victims. Argentina exfiltrated entire groups of executioners. Only in Buenos Aires could you have come upon Adolf Eichmann and

Josef Mengele enjoying a cup of coffee right next to Jewish patrons. If I'm calculating properly, my grandfather and Eichmann lived in the same city for seven years, between 1953 and 1960—that's roughly 2,555 days—, and this is enough reason for me to conclude they no doubt crossed paths multiple times. In a restaurant, a bakery, a square, some street downtown, at a shoe store or Harrods, on Florida Street, at the newsstand, at Cafe Tortoni or near Borges' table at La Biela. Maybe they bumped into each other by accident or simply made eye contact. It's even reasonable, statistically speaking, to think that one afternoon in 1953, without knowing it, my grandfather, Adolf Eichmann and Josef Mengele all ordered, at the very same moment, an espresso ristretto and an alfajor filled with dulce de leche in the little wood-panelled Zurich confectionery, perched in Belgrano, where my grandfather lived. As a child, I went to Zurich countless times to drink a cold glass of milk on beautiful summer days after playing in the square. My lack of education at the time spared me any dark associations.

3

I arrive at Porte d'Auteuil, on the edge of the Paris *Périphérique*. There's the sound of cars, of arrivals, departures: it's bustling for a Sunday. I step onto a little walkway behind the entrance to the metro station. It's almost nature: it's not nature. There are people running. I see workout clothes, headphones, the smell of sweat mixed with the fresh April wind brushes past me at intervals. Looking after your body is a possibility: I'd even say that it's a decision. I gave up on caring for my body a couple of years ago, when I stopped playing tennis for good. I made a mistake there: to care for your body is to keep yourself alive. I let myself get swallowed up by my thoughts and reasonings and I forgot my body, like I forgot my shoes. Maybe one day I'll start exercising again; that dream is possible. And yet, I think I'll never be able to go back to playing tennis or exercising in general. I would have preferred to forget my thoughts—not my body. It's true that exercise makes us forget many things. I think playing sports is forgetting yourself. Sports is a worthy pastime, not to be neglected. In my case, I neglected the practice of sports in general, and, well, I regret it everyday.

Sports were important to the Nazis. Hitler was committed to the Berlin Olympic Games he hosted in 1936. It was all there: Richard Wagner's "Homage March," the innumerable arms held up toward the sky, and the hope, of course, of winning. And not to forget the Olympic flame ceremony, which took place there for the first time. Today, we still perpetuate the myth of the flame. It comes to us from those 1936 games: it comes to us from the games so closely followed by Adolf Hitler. I thought I told you: everything is connected.

Now I'm in front of the racetrack; it's incredible. The whole journey, all those steps. A voice inside me speaks, tells me I've done it. My exhaustion is violent, it bites and burns me but I continue: I'll keep going until continuing becomes pointless. Don't ask me why. I don't know. It has to be nearly 2:00 PM. The cloud-covered sky is full of different shades, all layered on top of one another. They vary from almost black to almost white. In other words, rain seems inevitable to me but I can't say when it's going to fall, even if one thing is for sure: soon I'll be able to sleep. I mean: to flee through the door of dreams. The conclusion I gather from this thought is *forget the tiredness because it, too, will disappear.*

The entry to the Auteuil racetrack is an iron gate which creates a remarkable sense of delineation. There is "before the track" and "after the track," that kind of sensation. It's clearly born from the presence of the gate. The logic that follows from this sensation is the feeling that the racetrack is otherworldly. *I'm at the racetrack* is like saying: *I'm in another world.* I enter the Auteuil racetrack. People look, but no one questions me. I've just crossed the threshold, so I can now say: I'm in another world.

There's a paved plaza in front of the entrance to the stands. I'm in the plaza. I see a children's merry-go-round; it's a little carousel next to a crepe stand, like at the fair. The little carousel isn't turning yet. Maybe it won't turn at all today, on the Sunday of the big race, because there won't be enough children around. There has to be a significant number of children for the ride to be profitable. But sometimes I get it wrong. Look, a little blond boy lost in the lineups to get into the stands: I see him, he's behind his father, he's struggling to keep up, he doesn't seem very happy. He's there, he exists. I have clear ideas, it's only my vision that's blurry, as if my eyelids often give up for a moment before resuming their instinctive blinking—all of that in the space of two seconds. No, not blurry: my vision is jolting and twitchy, and so is my thinking. That toddler looks just like Balthazar did when he was five. Yes, I'm lying, my

nostalgia is playing tricks on me. They don't look anything alike, not at all. Bal had light brown hair and eyes
blue as the sea. As for me, I was blond as a wheatfield.
Time takes the glimmering things. Look at my hair
now, nothing remains of my blondness except for a couple coppery highlights at midday and a sun-bleached
halo around the edge of my forehead: that's all. That little carousel, if no one is around to repaint it, will also
end up tarnished. Rusted, even. But how would you ever
know? Right now it's there, it's shining, it's turning. It's
beautiful. I'll admit it, I adored carousels in the days
when I was still blond. Bal had eyes blue like the ocean,
not like the sea. The nuance is slight, but it's there. The
ocean is purer deeper darker, that's what I think.

If time had allowed, I could've taken ten turns,
fifteen turns, riding those wooden thoroughbreds.
Rising, descending, rising, descending, turning around
and around until dizzy. And afterward, an ice cream or
cotton candy. Never tired at the fair, you're alive, you're
intoxicated, you're winning all the games. Fishing hole,
shooting gallery, the coconut toss. Even the games you
lose you end up winning because you just play over
and over again. Stuffed animals, always stuffed animals. Candies, I gave them all to Bal, I never liked
candy. I believed in fairs. A universe overflowing with
promise! The goal: to win. Everything made sense. It's
the same with horse races. The goal: to win. And if you

lose, you play again. To be number one. At worst, number two, number three. Don't ask me why I love winning, I don't know.

It's almost nice out, I'm in a T-shirt, I surrendered my legendary jacket to the garbage can near the carousel. Just like that, I wanted to. I'll regret it one day. No, I never regret anything. If I'd been beaten as a child, how would I know? Yes—how can you know? I forget, I remember, I forget—until the vertigo comes. The merry-go-round near the Trocadéro, it was familiar, I can still picture it. Sundays before bath time I was allowed one ride. The bath: miserable. To wash, to undo yourself. Dirt was comfort. Close the past, Alma. I'll never be like you, I've just understood that.

I need to choose my horse, choose my number. I have to concentrate. I wanted to believe in the existence of a rigorous explanation concerning the meaning of my life. There, I made a mistake. That being said, I can give everything over to forgetting: it accepts everything. Yes, we will die, but we will always continue to dwell in the world of forgetting. I take the names I take the bodies I take the memories: I enclose them. It's an eternally memorable kingdom, I decide on that.

It's possible that I don't like solutions. Maybe what I want is to bathe in the ignorance and swim through the nothingness of this world's cruelty, I want the horse I choose to win the race, I want to feel a shiver the moment he crosses the line. Now I can say I'm a bit feverish, that I'm seeing red, that I'm agitated, nearly numb at the idea of a victory, and my nerves are on fire, I lied before: obviously I want to succeed, what more could I want! To succeed and to win are verbs that suit me. I'd even say they're certainly the only words I've always believed in. As far back as I can remember, everything has been about this. We don't have enough forests, I've just realized. Where's the forest near this track? Because after the race, we should be able to go dance all night in a forest—we'll call it the Auteuil forest—we only need to replant trees by the thousands, simulating a random and wild grove. "One More Time" by Daft Punk will be played on enormous speakers hung high from the beech trees, creating the illusion that music is falling from the sky. We could imagine the Daft Punk, we wouldn't necessarily have to really play it. We could reproduce it in our heads because it's simple: it's anchored in the memories of two generations.

I look at the people, their jackets. Quilted, waterproof, waxed; there's beige, Edgar-brown, navy blue, emerald green, and chartreuse. As for the fabrics, I can pick out corduroy and tweed, some wool, cotton, rayon, a few hats, some dresses, some brightly colored skirts in red, pink, and turquoise (those repulse me); and then there are berets, ties, polo shirts, and as for shoes, probably a mix of Berluti and Reebok.

§

Disappointed to see the storm approaching. The sky shrouds itself in darkness. Still, there remain a few small slivers of light. "The going is so springy! Let's hope the rain holds off until tonight, eh, Glory?"—an owner just passed behind me with his thoroughbred. He was energetically patting him on the neck. I smelled horse. Leather, oats, stables. I didn't feel anything. But I did see clearly. It lasted three seconds. It was strong, it was powerful, how to put it . . . it's impossible to explain. How to explain the feeling of lightning to someone who's never been struck? There's a limit to language, that's the real problem—I'll defer to the invisible. And besides, it's not that Glory was particularly noble or anything, but a horse has to have a way of carrying itself, it has to have a certain spark of greatness, as my uncle used to say. I went over to the information booth and stole a program. I open it, I'm going to choose my horse, I'm going to choose my number. The Grand Steeple-Chase de Paris race is set to start at 3:20 PM. Number of horses on the track: sixteen. The race is 5,800 meters, twenty-three obstacles. First, I look at the names of the horses, that's my priority. Then, the color of the silks. Finally, the names of the owners and those of the jockeys. I'm not a professional: I'm a being adrift. A bit like the leaf of an ash tree, covered in mud, losing itself as it flows along a river. I think of Wolfgang, only of Wolfgang, while I look over the names of the horses. His appearance, his grace, his possibilities—it all comes back to me. He's dead. I think it, I want to say it: it's scandalous. And then suddenly I see the seventh horse, his name begins with W, my heart skips a beat, my gaze is frozen, I raise my head toward the stands. I say out loud: "Werther du Soleillage: number Seven." Silks of blue and yellow diamonds. Werther du Soleillage. Wolfgang. Werther. Wolfgang.

The sun is not a planet. The sun is a burning star. A nuclear fusion reactor that's been working for five billion years, I'll never forget this sentence, heard in fourth grade physics. They were sleeping, they were passing notes, they were goofing around—I was captivated. Scientists aren't 100 percent sure that the sun will keep burning tomorrow: they can't promise that it will. Today, I'll see the sun burn. But the sun could go out: there could be a short-circuit. At this moment, I think that even if the sun suddenly stopped burning, the race would still happen. Because everyone is crazy: nothing is more important. Everyone has their horse, their number.

I went to see Werther du Soleillage in the presentation ring. He seemed respectable to me, possibly even a winner, I thought. Bay coat—the color of Edgar, golden in the light—alert gaze, a touch haughty, overall maybe a bit distracted, but I thought he was saving his attention for the obstacles. As for me—I'm saving my attention for the race. My last few blinks, a final sigh. Afterward, I might be able to sleep. I say "might" because I'm not sure I'll be able to close my eyes and put my brain on standby: to leave this night this day this world. It's been so long—it's not over—it went on for so long I thought I died. I didn't tell you, didn't tell you how much I really believed I'd died. I'm there now. I don't feel like I'm in reality, it's much more like I'm in the waiting room of a dream. It's possible that I'm sleeping: how would I know if I was sleeping? No, I'm awake—the field is in front of me. All that's left for me to do is to go fifty meters, fifty steps if I have it in me: I can do it, I'll be that bold. Don't want to be in the stands. They're too far from the action. I stop in front of the white railing at the edge of the course: closest to the horses. I smell grass, damp, fresh, trampled, bruised. The gardeners are patching over the places where the turf has been torn up. They advance in procession. There are five. Or four. They are three. I approach. I'm there, elbows resting on the railing. The photographers go out onto the field. They walk slowly, by force of habit.

§

April 4, 1943, at 2:16 PM. Do you remember? But how could you forget, yes, I remember. I knew thanks to that amazing invention—Google—how else would I have known? No one told me, no one told me the story. I saw pictures. People running. Lots of black and white. Lots of shells exploding in front of the stands, and even on the track. Seven dead. Forty wounded. It wasn't far from here: no, it wasn't far at all.

To lose your life at the races

Not just horses lose their lives at the races: seven human lives lost there too. Allied bombing: American. I'd bet my right hand that at least one of the pilots who executed the attack was nuts about baseball. A baseball fanatic killed a horse-racing fanatic. Look how everything is connected, always. For example: me, I love baseball, I love races, I'm here now. And I remember April 4, 1943, at 2:16 PM, a moment I didn't experience.

> *Suddenly, spectators and passers-by heard the sound of plane engines in the clear sky, and almost immediately bombs began to fall in seven or eight spots near the race track. The anti-aircraft batteries around the field immediately sprang into action, and the crowd, after a brief moment of panic, managed to take cover in the woods and a few nearby shelters. Alas! This day of fine sunshine and beautiful sport was also to be a day of blood and mourning.*

It was like I'd heard those lines on the radio, when actually I read them in a newspaper from April 5, 1943. The information is available, all you have to do is plumb the depths. And then, above all, wait: waiting is a beautiful thing, no matter what anyone says. I'm waiting for the race. I'm waiting for sleep, I'm waiting for love, I'm waiting for eternal life, I'm waiting to reunite with my dog, I'm waiting for bombs, I'm waiting for the end of all things. Have you believed anything that I've been able to tell you? No—I'm not waiting for anything. I abandoned expectation the day I threw my Labrador in the trash with his blue cushion. Everything begins to bore us eventually. Soon, I'll have my driver's license, I'll get a car, I don't care what color or make and I'll drive across France, across Germany, across Italy, and then I'll take a boat all the way to Cape Cod. Luckily, Americans drive on the right, I won't have to change cars. All I have to do is stay out of England.

The horses are ready. Under starter's orders. Exhaustion—the wave rises, it rolls in. I resist. I'm no longer in my body first and the world second. I'm first and foremost in the world. I see my horse over there, my Werther, my Soleillage. Striking how he resembles Wolf. It's not about the color: it's something in his manner. The group closes ranks. A last prayer for my number Seven. The starter brandishes the red flag, I see stars. And they're off.

Look now, I've noticed a baseball diamond in the distance, behind the racetrack. Baseball legend Lou Gehrig appears out of nowhere. *Alma, come back*, I murmur. My concentration has been jeopardized. But I really do see him, I swear. He's tall, he's wearing a striped gray and blue shirt, his Yankees cap, the glove on his right hand holds an immaculate ball, whose absolute whiteness is dazzling under the light of the sky. I tear myself away, I fix my eyes on the start gate: what is more seductive than the launch, the take-off: the beginning of a trial . . .

A simple hedge to start things off: a taster, a little warm-up, delightful deception. Beginning with sweetness to increase the suffering that comes later: perversion. The hedge makes you think the adventure will be a happy and peaceful one. The horses are already long gone and, at the second obstacle, the disillusionment is clear: a double fence, twice the height of the hedge; *mesdames et messieurs*, we call this a qualitative leap, but worse is yet to come—much worse: the bullfinch looms. In the stands, jaws are clenched. Death is there, always ready to burst out of nowhere; those extended necks are vulnerable, I think of Wolf, his shining magnificence, his unforgettable beauty, his performance and fatal fall . . . What a memory!

Werther's saddle pad is white like a baseball, and the Seven is black as an abyss. Our horses have just finished their first lap, that was all preamble. Now they're tackling the oxer. We have our first injury: number Fourteen goes down and ambitions are extinguished, maybe there'll be tears—a thought for the owner—but we move on, more than ever, the fire of faith burns. Prince Werther du Soleillage comes to the *Rivière des tribunes*: the thoroughbreds fly over the pond, it ripples and then explodes into a thousand droplets. This race is an art; furious splashes, the brutality of the trial and the lightness of the moment—violence courage mud poetry. Another little hedge, we call this one a break, a truce, a let-up. The horses head toward the right half of the track and out of sight, I fall back on the screen, on the trees, on the sky, on the future, I imagine all of it! The steeplechase is earth water fire, but the sky is a constant. Eighth obstacle, another bank jump. The steeplechase, I see it, green and gray. I feel torn apart! I'm waiting for the moment after: the heart-explosion and the liberation. The course becomes more complex, I want to be able to cry, the arrival of the brook obstacle disenchants the crowd—I'm afraid and so are we all, we're all scared as hell, scared senseless, united in our torment, eyes fixed on that green ring—I don't want to lose my horse, not this time, not again, not now!

We lose the only things we believed in

Werther, listen carefully, focus: don't leave me alone! If your heart and your tendons are strong, we should be able to hold on . . . The brook was easy, too easy for W. The next fence resolutely awaits us: to punish. The *Gros* open ditch—that's what it's called. Translation: *If you dare*. It's a hulking thing, brimming to its full height with cruelty, like some fake mountain—a feat of human prowess, and again I bow—but decidedly nothing is going to stop my beautiful champion: he clears it, landing like the engine of an Ariane rocket pulverizing the ground! The game continues, next jump, oh God, I've completely lost my cool . . .

Stone wall, are you going to send us falling into the nightmare somersault, painful reminder of impossible eternity?—yes we're going to die, and maybe the hooves carrying my hope will catch on those bricks—I say *no Werth* and I think *no Werth*: don't let this affront take you down! Be careful not to break our pact: you're forbidden to let me down! But in my heart of hearts I'm not worried anymore: 2,900 meters and not so much as a scratch. It's a triumph: I feel drunk, lulled by the whirlwind of speed and the rhythmic breathing of those nostrils—steam engines, frenzied carriages on a gravel road—jump, gallop, jump again, everything forgotten, even regrets! I see no more, I think no more, I renounce even my first day of this mad life, in the name of God—oh this fractured life! Take everything,

I offer up my soul, my heart, my meager tears, my hope.
My illusions like candy! Don't be shy, go on, take them
. . . And about the colors and destiny: I'm inventing
them. I falter and fall. That irresistible sleep is coming. *No, Alma, hold on.* I swear, I'm going to make it. I
said I didn't believe in anything, except maybe numbers—but I believe in this race. I think I have a chance
with number Seven and it doesn't matter to me if this
morning the clouds choke out the sun. There is enough
light, and my memory knows that star so well I can
summon it at will. A bay pulls away from the group, it's
not my number Seven. Number Three takes the lead,
followed by Six and Eleven.

The first shall be last

My horse isn't among the first, or among the last, he
hasn't made his move yet, he remains hidden in the
pack, waiting for the third and final stretch of obstacles. You've got to bide your time, scheme from your
corner until the right moment—until the *coup d'état.*
I think: *races are like politics, like chess, like success, like
love: you have to be in the right place at the right time.*
The jumps streak past like faces in my memory; we are
in a tunnel flecked with light. An exceptional home
run draws my attention to the baseball field for a few
seconds, but the player slips and goes down hard. He

gets back up; I plunge back into the race. Werther goes by at the speed of sound, he's gradually breaking away from the group. Don't cry victory yet, I'm not in a video game.

I've conceded that the world is going to end for some time now, but I'm only beginning to understand it. I won't disclose my most intimate feelings. I only want to tell you that I've loved baseball with the same passion that I loved my dog, and Chateaubriand, too, I loved (I swore I'd keep that hidden in the secret places of my soul). *Forget the* Mémoires, *move sports up in the ranking*: I bridled my enthusiasm. It was too extravagant!

I don't know how old I am

Lou Gehrig keeps hitting. The ball goes way too far, that's for sure, it's going to hit a bomb. Because I see bombs, too, falling over there, on the Bois de Boulogne. They're these little points falling from the sky. A deafening sound followed instantly by a plume of thick smoke. They're all on the field, sometimes they look over at me. There are Wehrmacht soldiers. SS officers. Planes fly by. There's Max Aue, there's my baseball players, there's the Daft Punk robots, there's Glenn Gould, they're all walking, but don't make it to me: their steps aren't taking them anywhere. But oh well, I think: *The race, Alma, the race—see it through to the end.*

I'm in this epic

Double fence, then hedge, and like time, my horses are coming back, the stands bark bellow roar, but me, I don't care anymore I'm elsewhere: Werther is a star a bomb a legendary meteor, Werther is my blazing sun, the shooting star bursting out of my eyes! Yes I believe in my horse, I believe in the victory that is materializing like a new love, my heart leaps and capsizes, I want so badly to be capable of love! Just 2,800 meters more to endure, and then maybe someone will reach out to touch me, just once, I'm not holding my breath but I hope, I wish, I'm taking risks: my fall is free and impassioned. Tongued. Limbed. My fall is golden and crowned with azure, it's the lightning bolt that makes me shiver—to love, to love, to love, how to free myself from this verb, these four letters, mischievous and unyielding, that torment me! Go on Werth, weave your way toward the sky like a reptile, as if you were slipping between the banks of a river. *Werther and Dorothéa are here to announce that they will soon be leaving earth leaving the sky: taking on the universe. They'll find a nice planet: B 610, B 611, B 613— and they'll have a prestigious neighbor. Blond like the sun, with horribly unkempt hair, a cerulean blue overcoat with red lining, like a treasure, and then the sword . . .*

Alma, calm down

Look at me: you're boring me, I forgive you. You don't like me, I forgive you. You like me well enough, I forgive you. You like me too much, I forgive you. You've forgotten me, I forgive you. You flatter me, I forgive you. You wound me, I forgive you! You get close to me, I forgive you. You leave me ... I forgive you. Calm! To be at peace with the world with loss with forgetting. The end of the race is coming, a mound of dirt, and it'll be over.

Did you believe me? *Over?* Hardly ... The mammoth is still ahead, mastodon and king of the obstacles. The *Juge de paix*: hidden from this side of the track at the 4,800-meter mark; I raise my eyes to the giant screen and I admire the leviathan. An enormous tree trunk, an interminable stretch of empty space, and to top it off, an elephantine hedge: a whole world in one obstacle. This time we're definitely screwed. I think about my horse's coffin, the wood I'll choose. Is it possible to bury your champion? We left Wolfgang in the dubious hands of the veterinarians, and where did he end up? He went *through the looking glass*, as my uncle would say. To Wonderland, to be squared and quartered. The *Juge de paix* is coming, the *Juge de paix* announces its presence, it's a silent peak, the stands are empty of screams—every detail of everything, of life: forgotten. Hovering outside of time—the *Juge de paix*!

Cleared it

Like a package at the post office: signed, sealed, and delivered. Werth and I have just gained access to an exclusive, forbidden sphere: the sphere of the almost-winners. It's flashy, flatters you into feeling special. I believe in this victory, soon I'll have earned my place for good—become a winner. I've grown taller: my pride stretches like a lion. Werther! My noble Duke. Courage perseverance tenacity: and, above all, desire. The reward will be unheard of, I promise . . . Sadly, and mercifully, we just lost a jockey who wasn't blue-and-yellow. Picked off, like a fly by the tongue of a starving lizard, at the twenty-first obstacle. A simple hedge! Stupid. Went down like Félix Faure, mid-act, and over such a small thing . . . We didn't even see the thing up close; happily, the screen was there to show us the body hit the ground. His horse continues on alone. No casualties, please: I don't want them to interrupt the race for any reason. Have you ever noticed, though, that sometimes there are deaths and the race isn't interrupted? That's the magic of it all! A horse can go down on the battlefield, and it changes nothing. No neutralization: you just detach, release. The horses sidestep slightly to go around, brushing past the unlucky one. No time for death; this idea amuses me. We can't allow emotion to steal the show: it has to be invisible if it wants to endure. I think: *like in war*. A soldier dies, the battle goes on. A horse race is not just one form of entertainment among

others. A horse race is an ordeal, a bit like the extermination of the Jews. They slaughtered, and continued
on. They couldn't allow for interruptions. They had to
see it through to the end, to the end of their reasoning
and their convictions. You have to see the race all the
way through to the end: surpass yourself. It's definitely a
form of athleticism. Number Six is gaining on my horse.
He's putting an unpleasant amount of pressure on him.
Werther falters slightly. I understand why my grandfather loved the races; he was reliving the tension of his
short-circuit. Six and Seven are now neck and neck.

Die Six

I hear a voice suddenly erupt from my memory, rising
like a twenty-five-foot wave, it's my mother's voice, it's
soft, it says to me: *Dorothéa, whatever happens, you have
to step aside, and let others go.* We're heading toward a
possible victory, Six has been outstripped. But it's still
too early to say. Werther! No joke, I've bet my life on
your gallop! How fragile she is, that Alma, and how
fragile her little life . . . Worn down and bruised like a
shoe. You can't imagine how she wanders, how much
she wants to be loved. She's playing the horn in a distant forest, the echoing her only response. Beaten and
cowed, she picks herself back up, dreaming of the end,
dreaming of a truce: the absolute encounter.

Tenderness

I entered life, I left life, I rubbed shoulders with death (yes, I've known death), and I lingered on, in fear of being neither weak enough nor strong enough to endure the flames. Our horses are returning, my Seven is aflame and as for me, I am burning—I'm disappearing bit by bit, caught in the fanaticism of the need to love . . . I'm not going to try to escape it, no, I'm going to let myself be swallowed in the deluge of my ardor—love, loving, illusion, again, the wheel, always: wielding your rage as a weapon against the wasteland of the world! I give, when you let me; I need a face, a voice, to be given a secret, and a pause. Colors full solid discernible. A word, a nuance, a haughty gesture, invisibly tender: two undreamed-of solitudes. Yes I have loved without being loved, yes I've wanted without being wanted, so I took the road along the trenches at dawn, skin smeared with mud, bile and ignorance, my crushed dreams beside me . . . I recited a melody to myself in the silence of my memory, the notes braiding together, and I wanted to be applauded but fear has bled me dry, and the pain of the little lies, their bullets lodged in all my promises—what an uproar, a revolt—carried off, like birds toward a new season. Oh Alma, old before her time . . . Please, clear me a path toward the past, I have shipwrecks to return to. What happened to my boldness, my youth, my violence?

Impetuous volcano that I was! That I still am! But I hid myself, disowned the person that I was, there behind the curtain of the dark. I renounced passion, the performer in me, why? It's time to restore what is likable, to open myself to something greater than sadness. I can handle it all. I just need one single revelation.

I'm waiting for the lightning

I'm not of winter, I'm not of fall, I'm not of spring, I'm not of summer, but a fifth season. Thrown into the world, I saw and then I understood. Now the game is in your hands, it's a kingdom written in signs: braille, conceived to forgive. The race blazes with flame, like today. One more. I count the obstacles the strides the dead. My wound is like new, come, touch it. I don't dispute the way things go: I leave the evil, the good, to entwine themselves, to drive the days, dynasties, joys, names, and the affliction. Where are my horses? I abandoned them. Too much wanting, it's killing me. For a victory: how many failures must we fabricate? Seduction ...

Werther takes the lead, he gets in position. I've waited so long for this moment. Now that it's here, it's even worse. Werth can no longer allow himself to fail: in the great heights of hope, the length of the fall is also inscribed. I'm in no condition to fall very far: too exhausted, I have to be let down easy. Do you hear me,

Werth? If you fail, I'll disown you. No number 3, no number 2, no: I want you to be the only one up there, like God. As far as the extermination goes, I think I don't have to worry. I won't be wiped out like my ancestors—it's always good to say it—I can live on races, parties, Pepsi, I am free to breathe without the gut-twisting fear of ending my days in a mass grave, killed by a bullet in the back of my head or by carbon monoxide, and that's enough of a reason to give due recognition to the US, as well as the English, the Canadians, and the French Resistance. I think we should raise our glasses, and, on that topic, I'd like to try being drunk for a whole year to see what it's like, without ever sobering up, without experiencing the crash. To travel travel travel through words and moments. To cover myself in stories. In laughter. To wander between empty bottles, into daydreams, into fictions. To sleep at home at night, in my lost home! To return and remain there. To envelop myself in rest. Whiskey in my tea, honey, a few drops of milk. Oh, Balthazar, how we laughed. We went wild in the evenings, and doubled down again every morning. From dare to dare, from screw-up to screw-up, you never went easy on me, I never went easy on you . . . Dumb kids, spoiled kids, cruel and chivalrous kids, ready to lay down our lives for victory! For a better score! Brats! You would have bet on number 6 today, anything to hurt me. But your arrows were dull, their poison wounding and

raw but not fatal. We saw our fair share of things . . .
Around Auteuil, in the pampas-covered wilderness of
our daydreams, and then on rue Jacob . . . Miserable and
sumptuous feasts, stifling parties, evenings that seemed
endless . . . We lived a fairytale, we traded roles back and
forth: prince and princess, hero and villain, king fairy
valet queen and servant, unloved orphans. Beauty and
the Beast . . . The Good, the Bad and the Ugly . . . Fights
with feet, hands, pillows, cushions, how many feathers
waltzed across the room . . . Grandfather, you would
have liked us.

I buried my experiences in the wreckage of my
memory: my mad and unrealized hopes, horses athletes cherished books, so many times read and reread,
my schemes my deliriums my impossible and unavowed
loves, my machinations, my thirst for glory for accom-
plishment for the unknown. Grandfather, help me,
reason with me, don't you see that I'm losing myself,
that I'm lost? Do at least the dead see us, even if no
one else does? I am killing time with the memory of
your absence. When I want evening: I turn off the sky.
When I want peace: I drown out the voices with my
silent shouts. Grandfather, turn around and listen: I
have so much to tell you, no matter the order of the
words, and if they collapse altogether, my gaze and my
fears will remain to be confided in you. I've kept everything inside, heroes races athletes illusions, novels and

dreams, fears desires scrapes. I'm offering you a piece of my soul, maybe the worst part, maybe the most insignificant! Grandfather: yes listen to me I'm speaking to you. I have walked across the waters of my past, at dawn on the beach, feet offered up to the cold sand; I waited for the tide, for it to take me quickly, I whispered my litany before the enormity of the open sea, I said: *In error we have reached the point of perfection.* More than anything, I wanted a mind, an intelligence, a heart, to accompany me through this interminable wandering, and as I grow old, too, through the years that fall away; and I still want that. But I am a storm forbidden to believe, deeply cursed. And you, grandfather, did you believe one day at all, in even the smallest of moments? Jacob, name of my name, blood of my blood, I did not know you, I never touched you—everything fled into the dark. If you could speak to me, if I could hear you! Joys defeats sufferings triumphs. I want to remain like marble upon the Earth, like the heart of the world, like the water and the sun: to be unending.

My ears open again, the sound of the stands explodes across my face, it's quick and wounding like a scratch. We're coming to the end, it snuck up on me. Wolfgang is definitely going to cross the finish line alone. A thousand meters left. I meant to say Werther but I don't know anymore. It could be Wolf. Maybe he's still alive, maybe he never died; maybe I've been wrong

about everything. Expelled and sent back by time . . .
800 meters. My seven accelerates, he breaks away. Joy
subsides thirst subsides passion subsides and even bore-
dom succumbs to the show. We are forever being pulled
back down, incapable as we are of keeping our emotional state, our feelings, afloat: caught in the eternal law
of gravity . . . The voices stir, Werth is the lightning that
will strike the finish line, the future is infinitely close.
600 meters. My eyes burn, dilated, drugged by the final
sprint.

Don't wake me up

If it's not a mass grave, I want to be told about the real
risk that faces me. I want to know about the worst thing
that could happen to me in the time in which I live,
in the circumstances and the environment that are my
own. Back then, I thought the worst was the empty bottle of Coke on the coffee table. That emptiness was my
death. My seven is now in the lead. It's in these last
seconds that everything will play out. I think I've out-
grown that fear. The worst is maybe that I'll lose, but
that I don't know it yet—yes, that I don't know, that
I'm the fool. I admire the expanse of my sleep-encircled
kingdom. I don't know why I came here. A book like
The Little Prince brought color into my life and maybe
without *The Little Prince* I would have hung myself the

way a seven-year-old child would hang themselves on the slats of their bunk bed with a little belt of fabric or leather: a childish belt. Six is making a strong comeback. They are neck and neck. *The Little Prince* was a kind world: I needed a kind world. It isn't going to rain. We need a kind world like we need a rest, a truce, between two rivers of blood. 5,700,000. Why. They're coming the ground shakes I tremble. The screams of the crowd the children's joy. I killed you, you dirty animal. Like you, I will die. The sky baseball the sun the horses. I forgive Hitler, I forgive the Nazis. Pain is blue-yellow. I'm lying why am I lying. Still forty meters still a few seconds. Why God. I do not believe I am alive. 5,700,000— plus the innumerable particles of dust. We are covered in ash. Make a little hole in the ash, a trace. The finish the winner the applause. The world has changed, there is no going back. The world—I see it as cinnabar red. Remember, grandfather, how beautiful it was! No, I beg you, do not be disappointed.

Frederika Amalia Finkelstein was born in the nineties in Paris to a French father and an Argentinian mother. She studied philosophy and has published three novels at Gallimard: *Forgetting*, *Survivre*, and *Aimer sans savoir, Être sans comprendre* (forthcoming in October 2023). Her passions in life include reading, writing, travel, and listening to and making music. She sometimes composes and sings under the name Alma Elste. She currently lives in Paris and is writing her next novel.

Isabel Cout is a translator pursuing graduate work in Comparative Literature at the University of Montreal. Her research interests include third generation Holocaust narratives (especially as they pertain to questions of social alienation, identity, and belonging) and the role of Holocaust survivor testimony in both archival and legal contexts.

Christopher Elson is a Carnegie Professor of French, Canadian, and European Studies in the Dalhousie Faculty of Arts and Social Sciences and the University of King's College. His research and teaching focus to a significant degree on connections between literature and philosophy. He is the co-author of *In the Name of Friendship: Deguy, Derrida and Salut* (Brill/Rodopi 2018). He has translated essays and texts by a number of contemporary poets and thinkers, including Jacques Derrida and Jean-Luc Nancy. His translation of Michel Deguy's *A Man of Little Faith* appeared with SUNY Press in 2015.